SPEED

Railers Legacy 1

RJ SCOTT
V.L. LOCEY

Love Lane Books

Copyright

Speed

Hard ice. Fast cars. Fierce love.

Hockey is as natural as breathing for Noah Gunnarsson. Growing up with two famous hockey stars as his dads, Noah has always aspired to join the Railers to continue the Lyamin-Gunnarsson legacy. With his degree done, it's time to live that dream; the first step is getting a spot on the team his dads played for. The second step is to pull on that dusky blue-gray sweater and make his fathers proud. His rookie year is bound to be a season of incredible highs and lows, but one of the biggest highlights is meeting Brody Vance at a fundraiser. Brody is the living epitome of a bad boy hiding his pain behind a devil-may-care attitude. As Noah struggles to keep one eye on the puck and not on Brody, it's only a matter of time before love collides with sport in a chaotic splash of media attention.

Racing driver Brody Vance has spent his life chasing speed and glory and is only points away from his first world championship when a devastating crash ends his season. Determined to make a triumphant comeback, Brody is blindsided by a diagnosis that forces him off the track for good. With his world flipped upside down, and family and fans questioning why he left, Brody hides his pain by pushing the limits and refusing to let anyone see the cracks. But after a chance meeting with a sweet, sexy hockey player turns into an unforgettable one-night stand, fate keeps putting Noah in his path. With his heart on the line and his body racing against time, Brody must decide if he's willing to risk it all for love—or if he'll let fear and pride leave him in the dust.

Speed is a steamy M/M romance with a hockey rookie living his family legacy, a bad-boy racing driver with secrets, media attention that would break even the strongest of men, an unforgettable one-night stand, a love that means risking it all, and a hard-won happy ever after.

Dedication

To my family who accepts me and all my foibles and quirks. Even the plastic banana in my holster.
VL Locey

Always for my family.
RJ Scott

RAILERS LEGACY

SPEED

RJ SCOTT
& V.L. LOCEY

Love Lane Books

ONE

Noah

MY PHONE ALARM WENT OFF AT SIX A.M. SHARP, BUT I'D been awake for at least an hour before the chiming started. I should've cancelled it when I woke up at quarter to five. My nerves had been slowly climbing for the past few weeks when I'd talked to reps from different teams as draft day approached. Now it was here, and after a quick fasting blood sugar test, I grabbed some juice from the fridge, threw open the curtains, and went out onto the balcony to stare spellbound at the Sphere at the Venetian hotel. Las Vegas lay spread out before me, glittering as only Sin City can glitter. Sipping a cold can of tomato juice as the warm desert wind blew over me—I tried to settle my anxiety, but yeah, that wasn't happening.

Today was the day. I'd been working my ass off for years on the ice to make it to this point. Sometime over the next two days, I'd be drafted by a pro team. I hoped. I wasn't a super religious person, not as my nana had been before she'd passed. Mama, as Pops had called her, had been super devout, so who knows, maybe all those prayers she had sent skyward as I'd fought tooth and nail through high school and college to prove a dude with diabetes could make it to the big leagues had paid off.

Whatever the case, I was here, and tonight I'd be seated in the amazing Sphere with my dads as my future was decided. Where would I go? I had three teams I'd like to play for if the hockey gods were being benevolent. I'd be happy to go to Boston or LA. Both the Rebels and Storm were good teams situated in great cities. I planned on spending four years in Bean Town playing for Boston College—Go Eagles!—while getting a theater arts degree. But my number-one choice after college would be the Railers. I mean, that was a no-brainer. My fathers had both played for the Railers, my biological father had been a super solid forward for Harrisburg, and my adoptive pop had been a Hockey Hall of Fame goalie. I'd grown up surrounded by legendary talents such as Tennant Rowe. As a fellow forward, sitting at a picnic table and talking hockey with Ten had been above and beyond. I'd learned so much from all the old guys, and now, after years of hard work, I would hopefully go home and show the GOATs just what I had.

As the sky on the eastern horizon began to pinken just a bit, I looked out over Las Vegas and found one of the songs I'd sung as the lead in *Oklahoma* in my senior year at school rolling around my head. I started belting out, "Oh, What a Beautiful Morning!" into a gusty wind pushing my sandy curls into my face as I made a small circle. Not to brag or anything, but I had a pretty good voice. I was no Hugh Jackman, but I had landed several leading roles during my school days. One of my teachers even said she felt I could make a go of it on stage if I applied myself, which was cool. I had a backup plan for when I couldn't play hockey anymore. Noah Lyamin-Gunnarson, the singing puck-pusher. I could see my name in lights on Broadway.

When I got to the line about cattle being statues, the sliding door to the room next door flew open with a crash. I instantly fell silent, hiding behind my can of tomato juice. An older guy, bald, with a big nose, leaned around the divider to glower at me in the predawn light.

"Is that you singing that stupid-ass song?" he asked, and I nodded. "Well, stop it. What kind of moron sings on a fucking balcony at the crack of fucking dawn? Why aren't you in a bar somewhere trying to get into some showgirl's panties?"

"Uhm, because I'm not really into showgirls. I mean, I date girls and guys, but I like the people I date to be—"

"Kid, I don't give a shit if you date donkeys. Stop fucking singing, or I'll call the front desk." With that, he disappeared, slamming the door.

"No one appreciates the arts anymore," I sighed as I finished the song but at a much lower volume. Chuckling to myself, I watched the sun rise fully. Then, I went inside to shower. I would need to eat soon, and my fathers would be up and ready at eight sharp. Earlier perhaps, as we were in Vegas, the city they'd been married in all those years ago. Plus, and this was huge, Vegas was Elvis central, and my Russian father was the biggest Elvis fan I had ever met. I could already imagine what we'd be doing today as we whiled away the time until the first-round picks were chosen this evening. I guess Elvis-themed hotels and tribute shows would take my mind off the most significant moment of my twenty-two years of earthly existence.

Man, I really *was* a good fit for a drama major.

But it was kind of true. My hockey life was about to be dictated by a bunch of old men sitting in a hotel room reviewing every player in this year's draft class.

No pressure at all.

If no one chose me, I could always hit the boards as Kenickie in an off-off-off-off-off-off Broadway run of *Grease* to put food on the table.

Man, I hoped a good team picked me. I'd look stupid with a DA hairstyle.

"HOW DOES ONE DAY DRAG ON FOR SO DAMN LONG?" I moaned into the mirror in my hotel room as I worked on looping a tie around my neck. My fingers were shaking. Not from anything to do with my diabetes but from straight-out nerves. Although the past twelve hours had been shit in terms of managing my condition. Stress always did this to me. The swings had been manageable for the most part. I'd felt pretty sluggish and muddled before lunch, but after a good meal and some time to chill at the Elvis Diner & Hound Dog Hot Dog Palace, I'd felt better.

Still, I'd better keep a close eye on my numbers. It would suck massively to be called for a round one pick— the odds of that were slim, as I wasn't a Cole Harrington or anything—to then faceplant as I went up to shake hands and get my sweater. To be honest, I doubted I'd be chosen tonight. Not that I wasn't good. I was pretty damn good, but I was no generational talent as Tennant Rowe had been, or Cole "Trick" Harrington III was this year. I'd be back tomorrow, Saturday, for rounds two through seven.

My tie was not cooperating, so I tied it into a bow and stalked out of the bathroom to find my jacket. As I passed, someone rapped on the door, so I detoured to check who was there. My siblings had not been able to make it, sadly, as Eva was home with some viral infection that had her spending the past few days puking and pooping. Pops said she'd probably eaten bad moose meat while camping with her fiancée in Ontario. My other sister, Margo, was over in Japan, working her little fingers away on an anime she and her boyfriend were producing for Animax. She and Botan were quite the team. While I wished they could be here, I totally understood why they couldn't. Sick was sick, and deadlines were deadlines. They'd be watching on TV, they assured me, as did my aunt Galina, who was nursing an impacted wisdom tooth.

What hurt worse was that my mother hadn't so much as called to wish me well.

Shaking that familiar hurt off, I opened the door to see my two fathers in the hall. Erik, my biological father, was spiffy as all hell in a dark blue suit that made his blue eyes pop. My adoptive pop, Stan, was dressed conservatively in an olive green suit that went well with his gray eyes. This look was subtle considering he'd been in an Elvis jumpsuit all day.

"Why is your tie in bopeep around your neck?" Pops asked, striding in to my room to stand before me. Pops was a big man so I had to tip my head up to stare at him. "Is this new trend for young peoples to make tie like birthday present?"

"Nah, I was just too jittery to get it tied right," I confessed. Dad inched in, worry on his face. "It's cool. My numbers are solid. I'm just really feeling all the nerves. What if I don't get a team I like?"

"You'll go to a team you love, I'm sure," Dad said, then nudged Pops and his big fingers aside to undo my tie. "Even if you don't, lots of players go to teams they don't think they'll enjoy, but they then find that the team, city, and fans make things better. Now lift your chin."

I could do this myself, obviously but there was something comforting about having your daddy fuss over you. And man, could these two fuss. They were both fussers extraordinaire.

"Da, your dad is right. It will all be good as gumdrops," Pops assured me as he loped to the sliding doors to stare at the Sphere. "Is most amazing thing that big orb. I wish Mama were here to see it. She would like it."

"Yeah, Grandma would have been super proud," I said, and Dad gave me a soft nod and smile as he whipped my tie into shape, then patted it. "Mom hasn't called yet."

Dad frowned. "She will. You know your mother. She tends to get caught up in herself but, eventually, remembers there are other people to think about."

"Yeah, I know." And I did know that. It's funny how, no matter how old you are, a slight from your parents hurts worse than any other kind. "So, hey, this is a happy night. Let's head over and face my future!"

"That is spunky pep talk! You will make good captain

one day, little rabbit." Pops draped a thick arm over my shoulder, tugged on the lapel of my navy suit, and pecked my head.

Captain talk was a giant leap. Right now, I'd be happy to be chosen at all.

It was a short distance to the venue, so we walked, the desert air making me sweat. Pops and Dad chattered the whole while. I was usually talkative, but this was too big of a moment, and my nerves were shot.

The coolness of the air-conditioned interior made me feel less twitchy. The armpits of my shirt were already damp, as was my collar. I should've cut my hair, but I liked it on the long side. My curls, courtesy of Dad, would look pretty epic hanging out of the ballcap the Railers GM would put on my head. If all went as I hoped. Let's face it, flow was important.

The room where the draft was held was massive, with chairs on higher risers for the players and their families. On the floor, hundreds of NHL reps milled about tables set beneath a giant domed ceiling with the logos of each pro team.

I felt my guts tighten as our faces replaced the logos— hundreds of hopefuls on that massive screen. I found mine. I looked as goofy as I felt.

"This is big day," Pops said by my ear. I nodded dully. I was caught between being excited and terrified. "If you need sugar snack, just shout. We both have pockets filled."

"Thanks, Pops," I whispered. Someone called my name. I found a familiar face, then another, and then another. "I see a few friends," I told my fathers as we made our way to our seats.

"Go and talk to them. We'll save your seat," Dad said with a smile.

Lots of bro hugs. A small group of us from eastern division teams were shooting the shit, talking about where we hoped to play, girls, guys, and parents, when the prime cut of this year's draft sauntered up. Cole Harrington III—Trick, to the rest of us mere mortals—strolled in with a woman on his arm who shut the whole room up. Dyna Bubble Mint. Yeah, that Dyna—the rapper whose debut track went gold two months ago. Apparently, first-round hopefuls get first pick of the rising stars, too. Still, I'm shocked she's on Trick's arm. Considering Trick's dad was a fire-and-brimstone TV evangelist with a holy crusade against anything queer or trans, it's honestly wild that Trick's even allowed within ten feet of Dyna.

"Hey, Trick," I said as he neared.

With Dyna on his arm, he strutted right past, as if he didn't know me or the other guys. We all watched them stroll on by.

"Okay, dude, that was rude," I grumbled at Trick's back.

He surely heard me but continued to his seat, an entourage following in his wake—not one of them looking like they were his parents. I shot the rest of the guys in my little chat circle a glance. They all shrugged. We all knew Trick was an asshole at times, probably inherited from his dad, and we'd all heard his homophobic shit—again, probably genetic. Sure, he had stupid skills. But no matter how good he was—and the shithead was good—he would be going to the worst team in the league. So sure, be smug, but not *that* smug. Most hockey players were humble to the nth—it was drummed into us from peewee up. Even great talents like Crosby, McDavid, and Madsen-Rowe were always respectful. They didn't walk around with their noses in the air. They were salt of the earth, as the play-by-play guys liked to say.

"Hope he has fun playing to the fifteen Atlanta Phantoms fans who are showing up to watch them lose," Craig Smythe, a hella nice guy and winger from Harvard, sneered. Being little brats, we all nodded. If anyone could use a good comeuppance, it was Trick.

"Truth," I added.

"You think he knows that Dyna is…" Craig waved at his crotch and then blushed when I raised an eyebrow. He knew Margo, my sister, had transitioned. "I don't mean… I just meant… fuck… his homophobic ass is going to be shocked when he finds a…" again with the crotch waving. I stared at him, humored him, and he slunk in his seat. "Fuck, I didn't mean that, I meant… Jesus… I'm shutting up now."

"Probably for the best," I deadpanned, and then shoved Craig. Hard. He ducked his head, still bright red, and muttered another sorry. He was a nice guy—more than that, really—and I knew he didn't mean any harm, but he needed to understand that it wasn't okay to reduce people to parts or labels like that.

When the lights dimmed, we all wished each other good luck and returned to our seats. I was wedged between Pops and Dad. My right leg began jumping. I could feel my tension creeping up, although I was sure I'd not be chosen tonight. The extra day of waiting was going to be torture, but we all sat through it. We clapped at each announcement, even Trick, who was grabbed up by the Atlanta team as predicted. The night was long but enjoyable.

"You will go second round for sure, I am predicting," Pops said as we made our way to our hotel around midnight. I'd been feeling lethargic, so we'd headed out after the final pick of the first round had been called up.

I bobbed my head in agreement. Second would be cool. Third fine. Fourth totally acceptable. Hell, lots of great players had been drafted low. A famous New York goalie had been a seventh-round pick, and he had made a name for himself that had gotten him into the HHOF.

I hit the sheets early, curling up to rest and talk to Rachel Biggs, my ex-girlfriend from college. She and I had dated throughout our junior and senior years, but as graduation had gotten closer, and my departure from Boston grew nearer, she began to see a future where she would be alone *a lot* if I did go pro. And all respect to her, she broke things off as gently as she could. I got it. The sig others of pro athletes were a special breed. They spent so much time alone, holding down the fort and raising kids. Shit, I wasn't sure I'd want that kind of life if I weren't an athlete. So yeah, Rach and I were still friends.

She was also a theater major packing up to move to Manhattan. We talked about that for a long time, and her cat Mojo, and her little sister who was still crushing on me, she said. When I yawned in her pretty face, she gave her long, dark hair a flip, played all affronted, and told me to get some sleep. She wished me luck, blew me a kiss, and ended the call.

Sleep was elusive that night, but it finally came after I

recited the script from *MacBeth* in my head. I conked out at the line about my dull brain, which was on track.

The next morning, I was up early, took a swim instead of singing to greet the day, and met my fathers for breakfast at the hotel restaurant. I had an omelet, bacon, and some sautéed mushrooms. Coffee with a shot of milk that I had to count for my daily carb intake, but fuck it, I liked milk now and again. Even the most dedicated low-carb follower gave into temptation. Not like it was a milkshake. Those were my Achilles heel. Nothing lured me to the dark side like a chocolate shake.

After the meal, we changed into suits and returned to the vast, domed room for rounds two through seven. It promised to be a damn long day for guys who weren't chosen until the last round or not at all, which happened. I hoped that wasn't my fate.

Thankfully, it wasn't. At ten forty-five in the morning, June 28th, three weeks after the Stanley Cup final, I was picking at the hem of my shirt sleeve when the Railers reps filed onto the stage. My attention moved from my sleeve to the man holding a Railers jersey on stage. We were into the third round now, and as soon as my face and stats flared brightly on the screen behind the Railers people, Pops shouted in glee. I blinked twice to ensure I was seeing what I was seeing and not having a low-sugar fantasy.

Nope, it was me. Sixty-fourth overall. Not too shabby.

I rose as the crowd applauded, hugged my teary-eyed fathers, and made my way to the stage. A showgirl in a sparkly silver outfit took my jacket. I jogged up the stairs, shook hands with people, and then, pulled that famed dusky blue and gray sweater over my head. Someone–the GM, I think–plunked a hat down on my head. Pictures were taken. I was led off the stage to schmooze with Railers' upper management.

"Welcome to the team, Noah," Tristen Routers, the Railers' new owner, said as we waited for my parents to join us backstage. "You're planning on going to college, right?"

What did he want me to say? Did he want me to go straight to the team? I wasn't ready. I wanted an education, something to fall back on. Was I messing this up from the start? I caught sight of my dads coming into the room and straightened my back at the pride in their expressions.

"College, sir," I answered.

He laughed, then pressed a hand to my shoulder. "Good call."

I wanted to get my degree, make the team in the big show in four years, or go to the Colts, our AHL feeder team. I wanted a career as a hockey player, so it was back to the ice as soon as I got home to train my ass off, then hope I stood out to Coach Morin—if he was still there—in four years.

TWO

Brody

Four Years Later

IT WAS LIKE THAT WEIGHTLESS MOMENT IN A RACE CAR when you take a curve too fast—just for a second, you feel like you're flying, like the world has tilted in your favor and gravity forgot your name. Adrenaline hums in your veins, the engine roars beneath you, and you're suspended in that split-second illusion of control. Then, just as fast, reality slams back in—you skid, you spin, you crash back to earth, heart in your throat, breath stolen, and all that fleeting hope burns out on impact.

"I'm sorry, Brody."

Dr. Reilly's voice was a hammer driving nails into my chest. I stared at the man, his words failing to sink in, bouncing off the walls of my skull as if they were in someone else's story. A diagnosis. *Concerning.* My stomach twisted tighter and tighter, but I just sat there, numb.

"Maybe you're misreading it?" I tried to keep my tone

as level as his, not letting one bit of my internal horror spill over.

"The MRI doesn't lie, Brody."

Logan's hand landed on my shoulder, grounding me, the faintest squeeze telling me he was there. Always there. I didn't look at him, couldn't. I kept my eyes on Dr. Reilly instead, hoping I'd misheard.

"A brain aneurysm," the doctor continued, his tone infuriatingly calm. "It's small, but it's there. Right now, it's asymptomatic—aside from some of the emotional volatility you've been experiencing, which is common. But I must be clear—this condition means you can't race again. The risks—"

I held up my hand. I didn't need to hear the rest.

Risks. Consequences. I knew all about those. I lived with them every time I strapped myself into a car. But this? This wasn't part of the deal.

"This must be a mistake," I said, my voice hoarse. "I feel fine. I don't even have a concussion, for Christ's sake."

Dr. Reilly exchanged a glance with Logan, but my brother didn't say a word. Not yet.

"Your body took a significant impact, but this isn't about the accident."

I shook my head, trying to clear the fog. The crash. Right, the crash.

Las Vegas Grand Prix. I was only ten points away from my first world championship. All eyes were on me. Turn 14.

I was flying—two hundred mph, maybe more—when I hit the brakes—a fraction of a second too late. Just one miscalculation, a razor-thin error, and the car skidded out, slammed into the barrier, crumpling around me like a soda can. I didn't even recall the impact, just the sound of carbon fiber screaming before the marshals pulled me out.

Drivers crash all the time. Race cars are built to survive it. I was bruised, sore as hell, but whole. *Not even a concussion.* I was supposed to walk away. Get back in the car. Finish the fight for the championship.

"But why—"

Dr. Reilly held up a hand. "This aneurysm didn't develop overnight, Brody. It's likely been there for some time, undiagnosed."

"This is fucking bullshit!" I shot forward in my chair, fists clenched so tight my knuckles burned, and for a split second, I wanted to dive over the desk and beat this asshole to a pulp. How dare he sit there as if he wasn't single-handedly ripping my world apart?

"You don't know me," I growled, my chest heaving. "I'm fucking Superman!"

Logan shifted beside me and rested a hand on my arm in warning, but I didn't care. My vision narrowed on Dr. Reilly; his expression infuriatingly composed, as though I was just another name on a chart. I wanted to see fear on his face.

I wanted to tear him down with every word, to intimidate him into choking on his diagnosis, and scare him so bad he'd scramble to take it all back. He was talking, using words like *asymptomatic*, *risk factors*, and *rupture*, but I wasn't listening. His voice was just background noise, a droning buzz that didn't matter, not when my entire world was crumbling. I couldn't hear the death sentence or process that everything I'd worked for—bled for—was slipping through my fingers.

Not now. Not when I was so close to showing people how fucking good I was. Not when I was just points away from proving I belonged at the top, that all the sacrifices, the sleepless nights, and the endless hours on the track had been worth it.

I stared at this expert who thought he knew me, my vision tunneling as his mouth kept moving, but none of it reached me. I couldn't hear him over the screams in my head telling me this couldn't be happening. Not to me. Not now.

I gripped the edges of the chair so hard my fingers ached, my mind racing through every excuse, every argument, every reason why this had to be a mistake. Because if it wasn't, then what the hell was I supposed to do? If I wasn't Brody Vance, the bad boy who lived and breathed speed, then who the fuck was I?

"This isn't happening," I snarled, interrupting him mid-flow. "I'm fine. I *feel* fine. I don't care what some stupid MRI says—I'm not stopping. Not for you. Not for anyone."

Logan's voice cut through the rising storm in my head. "Brody—"

"Don't," I barked, whipping my head toward him. "Don't you dare try to back him up. You're supposed to be on my side!"

"I am on your side, little brother," Logan said, his tone even but laced with a quiet intensity that cut through my anger. "But this? This is going to kill you if you don't listen."

Fury roared in my chest, a fire I couldn't extinguish. I turned back to Dr. Reilly, my jaw tight, my voice dropping to a dangerous growl.

"You're wrong," I said, each word sharp and bitter. "I'll prove you wrong. You'll see."

Dr. Reilly didn't flinch, his steady gaze meeting mine. "This isn't about proving anything. Look, Brody, I'm not your enemy. I'm trying to save your life."

I laughed bitterly, the sound scraping my throat. "Save my life? You're destroying it."

"Shut the fuck up, Brody." Logan's voice cut through the haze. "Listen to him."

My brother's pale gray eyes locked onto mine. There was no judgment in his expression, no anger. Just the weight of someone who'd been through hell with me before and was ready to do it again.

"I don't need to listen to this," I muttered, looking away. "I'm fine."

"No, you're not." Logan's hand dropped from my shoulder, but his voice stayed steady. "This isn't about being tough. You can't race again, Brody."

The words hit harder than the crash itself. Harder than any of the 4g forces I'd endured on turn 14. Racing wasn't just something I did; it was who I was. And now?

I felt the first crack in my armor, and I hated it.

Dr. Reilly cleared his throat, his tone maddeningly calm, as if he weren't delivering a death sentence on everything I'd built my life around. "I know this is a lot to process. Take some time. But you need to understand —racing would be catastrophic, Brody. The combination of high g-forces and the stress on your body could cause the aneurysm to rupture. It's not just dangerous. It's fatal."

Fatal. The word hit me like a punch to the chest, but I forced myself to shove it aside, bury it under the blinding, white-hot anger that was my constant companion.

"You're legally bound to keep your mouth shut," I said, my voice sharp, daring him to disagree. "Patient confidentiality, right?"

"You're correct," Doc said. "I won't share this information without your consent."

"Good," I snapped. "Then this conversation is over. I'll slap an NDA on you and anyone else who knows if I have to."

"Jesus, Brody," Logan snapped, and I yanked my arm from under his touch.

"Brody." Doc was louder, his tone hardening.

"What!"

"Do you want your legacy to show that you killed other drivers because you died at the wheel?"

The words felt like a slap in the face. My hands curled into fists, and my breath quickened as his question lingered, suffocating me. Legacy meant everything, but my legacy was a championship, pulling myself out of hell and becoming the man no one expected me to be.

"Don't," I growled, my voice low and full of venom. "Don't you dare try to guilt me."

"It's not guilt," he replied firmly. "It's reality. You think you can hide this, but the truth will come out, one way or another. Do you want that to be what you're remembered for?"

I glared at him, every muscle coiled like a spring. I

hated him. Hated the calm, logical way he laid out my nightmare as if it was some goddamn PowerPoint presentation. But as the rage burned in my chest, his words burrowed in, the truth of them leaving cracks in the wall I was so desperately trying to shore up.

I didn't answer. I couldn't. I just sat there, silent and seething, as my world crumbled around me, and I clenched my fists to stop the shaking. This couldn't be happening.

"Give us a minute, Doc," Logan ordered.

Dr. Reilly nodded and left the room, the door closing behind him.

I stared at the blank wall, every muscle in my body tense. "This isn't happening, Logan. I can't—I won't stop. Racing is my life."

"No," Logan said quietly. "Your life is more than racing, Brody. And it's not over. But if you don't stop... it could be. I won't lose another brother."

I yanked my arm from his. "That's fucking low, even for you."

"Jesus, Brody..."

I couldn't look at him, but his words sank in, carving through the denial like a scalpel. I hated him for saying it. And I loved him for being the only one who could.

For the first time since turning fourteen, I was scared.

Terrified.

THREE

Brody
<hr>

WASHINGTON BLURRED PAST THE TINTED WINDOW, AND I leaned back against the leather seat, trying to tune out the soft hum of conversation.

I was here for my niece.

My sister-in-law, Sadie, sat beside Logan, her voice calm and steady as she reviewed the event's details again, the picture of composure. As the daughter of a diplomat, she'd grown up in a world of fundraising galas and high-profile gatherings, and after Avery's diagnosis with Type 1 diabetes at the age of two, she threw herself into advocacy and fundraising as a way to cope, turning her grief and fear into something tangible. Sadie had a way of commanding attention without ever raising her voice—a quiet confidence that drew people in and made them listen. Nights like this? They were her domain, and she handled them as if she were born to it.

People were drawn to Sadie because of her warmth and charm. And Logan? He was the rock—the reliable one who always had the answers.

Me? I was just the guy in the window seat, pretending not to notice the occasional glances Logan shot my way.

The truth was, I didn't want to be here. This wasn't my world anymore. I was the face people recognized that sold tickets—the name that would get headlines for a cause I cared about.

It was about the only thing I cared about.

Logan and Sadie had the real reason for the galas, speeches, and fundraisers. They were trying to create a world where kids like Avery didn't have to deal with needles, blood sugar monitors, and the fear that one bad day could lead to disaster.

I respected the hell out of them for it. But that didn't make me any less bitter about being dragged along. I'd done my time in the spotlight for far too long, part of the insanity not due to being a driver but having dated world-famous singer Jemima Wren.

We'd only lasted a year—both focused on our careers—but we'd parted on good terms and were still friends.

Should I tell her what was happening?

Why would she want to know? She's your ex.

I don't want her pity!

"You'll need to make more of an effort tonight, Brody," Logan said, his voice cutting through my thoughts. "You're getting a reputation for being obnoxious."

"Not my idea of fun," I deadpanned because that accusation hurt, even if I was an obnoxious bastard.

Logan's tone sharpened. "We're not doing this for fun, Brody.! We're here for Avery."

I turned to him, my jaw tight. "You think I don't know

that? Why the hell do you think I even got in this damn car?"

"You're acting like you're being dragged to your execution," he shot back, his gray eyes narrowing. "This is about something bigger than you, for once."

My fists clenched on my lap, the leather creaking under my grip. "Bigger than me? You don't think I know what that's like? My whole goddamn life has been about something bigger—fuck you!"

"Stop!" Sadie snapped, but her husband—my idiot brother—wasn't listening.

He leaned forward, his expression hard. "Well, poor Mr. Millionaire. You could start by not acting like the world owes you something just because you got dealt a bad hand."

"Fuck you," I snapped, the words out before I could stop them. "You think I like this? Do you think I enjoy sitting around waiting to see if my brain decides to kill me? I went to see Doc last week, okay? You know what he said? More waiting. More watching. No answers. No solutions. Just me, stuck in limbo while everyone else gets to move on with their lives."

Logan paled, and I could see the regret in his expression, but before he could start all the typical bullshit, I held up a hand. "Don't you dare pity me, you asshole!"

"Enough. Both of you," Sadie snapped.

Her words hung in the air like a lifeline, cutting through the tension threatening to choke us. Logan leaned back, exhaling, and I slumped against the seat, exhausted, pressing fingers to my temple where a headache threatened.

"Are you okay?" Logan asked because he was watching me and asked me that same question every move I made.

I dropped my hand.

"That's a relative term," I murmured.

Sadie shifted uncomfortably, glancing at Logan. I didn't have to see her face to know she silently told him to ease off. But Logan was like a dog with a bone when it came to me.

"Did he say there was any news about what's next?"

I turned to look at him, my jaw tight. "There is no 'next.' They keep watching, and I keep living with a time bomb in my skull. That's it, Logan. That's my life now."

Silence filled the car, heavy and oppressive. Logan didn't say anything, but I could feel his disappointment, his frustration. He didn't get it. He couldn't.

Sadie glanced between us, her tone softening. "You both need to stop taking it out on each other."

She was right. Logan wasn't the enemy here.

"He needs to back the fuck off," I snapped.

"And he needs to—"

"Enough!" Sadie snapped at Logan, and for a moment, I felt smug, then she turned to me. "You too!"

The rest of the ride passed in heavy silence. I knew Logan was getting tired of my shit. Hell, I was getting tired of my shit. But I didn't know how to fix it.

The limo slowed to a stop, the grand entrance of The Hay-Adams glowing in the golden light outside. The buzz of conversation and the flash of cameras seeped into the car, but none of us moved.

I wish I'd managed to slip under the radar here in the

States. Sure, America was home, but F1 didn't capture attention the way NASCAR did. While dedicated fans followed every race, the average American would recognize a NASCAR champion over an F1 driver any day. Anonymity here could have been a blessing, but I'd ruined that by dating Jemima—a popstar, Insta-goddess, and fashion icon who was constantly in the spotlight. Being labeled "Jemima's ex" stuck with me long after we split. For a time, I'd loved the attention that came with being on her arm, reveling in the envy and adoration we attracted.

But that was then, when I was younger, cockier, and naive enough to think fame meant happiness. Now, the spotlight felt suffocating. It wasn't just the intrusive headlines or constant speculation about my personal life— it was the loss of control, my story shaped by others without my consent.

No matter how hard I tried to escape, that world kept pulling me back. The press speculated endlessly about my retirement; social media analyzed every move. Wherever I went, whispers followed: "Brody Vance—Jemima Wren's Ex."

Truthfully, I wasn't sure how to reconcile my past self with who I was now. Before, the crowds and cameras had fueled my drive to succeed. Now, they felt like a burden, a constant reminder of everything I'd lost and of someone I wasn't sure I wanted to be anymore.

"Smile for the cameras," I muttered under my breath. Before I could reach for the door handle, Logan leaned over, his hand landing on my arm.

"I'm sorry," he said, his voice quieter than I expected.

I nodded, still staring at the tinted glass. "It's all good."

"It's not," Logan pressed. "I worry about you, Brody."

I let out a slow breath and turned to meet his gaze. His pale gray eyes—our dad's eyes—were filled with a mix of frustration and something else I couldn't quite place.

"I get it," I said, my voice as soft.

He hesitated, squeezing my arm briefly before letting go. "I love you, little brother."

I swallowed hard, and my throat tightened. "I love you too." A small smile tugged at the corner of Logan's mouth, and I mirrored it. "You, Sadie, and Avery—always. Okay?"

Logan nodded, leaning back in his seat. "Okay."

I drew a deep breath, letting it fill the empty spaces the argument had left between us. "So, let's do this thing."

He grinned now, a real one, and opened the door, stepping out into the cool evening air. I followed, the cameras flashing, the hum of voices growing louder.

I squared my shoulders and put on a smile. For Avery. For Logan and Sadie.

It was time to play the part. Again.

TWO HOURS INTO THE NIGHTMARE OF NOISE AND LIGHT, MY headache had—thankfully—eased, but the endless swirl of voices were all too much. The questions and faux-earnest commiserations didn't help either.

I kept trying to steer the conversations back to my niece and why we were all here tonight—raising awareness for juvenile diabetes. But somehow, every single person seemed more interested in *me*. Was I dating Jemima again? Why had I stopped racing? What was I going to do now? When would I make my big comeback?

How pissed was I that I missed being world champion by only twenty-three points? Not that they used the word pissed, they asked if I was disappointed.

Nah. Not me. I wasn't disappointed.

I was devastated. Destroyed. Lost. As though everything I'd worked for, everything I'd sacrificed for, had slipped through my fingers at the finish line. Twenty-three points felt like a lifetime, and no one would ever know how much it tore me apart, how every second of every day felt as though I was trapped in the wreckage of turn 14, unable to climb out or breathe.

But sure, *"disappointed"* worked just fine for them.

I had too many lawyers and PR reps on retainer to let the truth slip out. And even if I could say it, even if I wanted to, how could I explain it to them? That I'd quit to stay alive? That I was living every day with a countdown I couldn't see or hear?

I couldn't do it.

"I'll be right back," I mumbled to the couple standing before me, neither of whose names I'd managed to catch. I didn't wait for a response before turning and heading for the exit.

Striding purposefully through the crowd, I avoided eye contact and ignored the murmurs of my name. If I appeared focused enough, people usually wouldn't stop me. Instead of heading toward the bathroom signs, I veered off course, ducking under a velvet rope into a section marked *Private*.

The first unlocked door I found led to a small, dimly lit lounge. Old oil paintings lined the walls, and the worn-out elegance screamed exclusivity. I stepped inside, shutting the door behind me with a *click*, and leaned against it momentarily, letting the tension bleed out of my shoulders.

At least I wasn't giving a speech tonight. Small mercies.

I crossed the room to an overstuffed leather chair, sank into it, and let my head fall against the cushion.

For the first time all night, I let out a slow, shaky breath and allowed myself to slump. This wasn't how I wanted to spend the rest of my life—hiding, lying, pretending. But what other choice did I have?

"Um… hello?" The voice came from the far corner, startling me enough to make me jerk upright in the chair.

"Jesus!" I snapped, my heart racing as I glared.

A man stepped out of the shadows, and I blinked. He was slim but solid, with golden curls that looked as if they belonged on the cover of a magazine, and striking green eyes that widened as they locked onto mine. He wore a penguin suit like me, except his jacket was slung over his arm, a small pride pin glinting on the lapel. His shirt was unbuttoned at the collar, his tie loose as if he'd been fighting with it all night.

"You're Jemima Wren's ex! Hell, you're Brody Vance," he said, almost like a question, as though he couldn't believe it.

I went on the defensive, standing up from the chair. "What the hell are you doing in here?"

He held up a clear zip bag with bottles and a needle inside, and my stomach dropped.

My chest tightened. A druggie. Great. This night just kept getting better.

"Get out," I barked, my voice sharp and full of disgust. "And take your fucking drugs with you."

The guy froze, blinking as if I'd slapped him. "Insulin," he said, holding the bag higher as if it would stop me from throwing him out on the spot. "It's insulin. A needle for an emergency, testing stuff. I-I'm here for the event. Well, my dads are here. They played hockey…" He trailed off, motioning toward the bag. "I play hockey," he added, sounding flustered.

I stared at him, trying to make sense of his rambling. He shifted, patting his chest where I could now see a small, round disc stuck to his skin.

"I, uh, messed up with my readings earlier. I'm trying my chest for the first time, but it doesn't work as well as my arm. I just needed somewhere quiet to get my blood sugar under control." His words tumbled out in a rush, and he ran a hand through his curls, clearly embarrassed. "I-I can find another room if this is… I mean, I didn't mean to interrupt your…" He waved toward the chair where I'd been slumped moments ago, his gesture awkward but apologetic.

I stared at him, still processing. My anger simmered, but now it was mixed with something else—confusion, maybe even a little guilt. I'd jumped to the worst possible conclusion without thinking.

He was someone trying to handle his shit. It's the same as me.

I sighed, rubbing a hand over my face, the tension in my chest loosening a fraction. "No, it's fine," I muttered, stepping back and sitting down. "You don't need to leave. Sit down if you need to."

His shoulders relaxed, but his wide eyes stayed on me, cautious but curious. "Thanks," he said, moving to the far side of the room and sitting on the edge of a chair, fidgeting with the bag.

"Do you need me to get you anything?"

He brightened. "Oh, no, it's all good."

The small room fell into an awkward silence, and for a moment, I didn't know what to do with myself. Finally, my earlier anger faded into a strange exhaustion.

The night wouldn't be a complete disaster if I could hide here with the sexy man who wasn't a drug addict.

"I'm Noah," he said, setting his jacket over the back of the chair before extending his hand.

I stared at it for a second, then shook it. "As you said, I'm Brody."

"I know," he said with a small, nervous laugh. "Sorry, I'm flustered. It's not every day I meet a real-life racing driver."

"Former," I corrected, the word sharper than I intended.

"Oh, yeah," he said, his cheeks tinged pink, the color blooming across his face. Pretty. "Well, still." His voice was breathless as if he was trying to play it cool but couldn't hide the awe underneath. It wasn't just the words —how his eyes lit up, wide and sparkling, as if standing in front of something larger than life. I could feel the quiet hum of excitement between us and his unspoken thrill of being close to someone he saw as powerful and untouchable. It wasn't something I'd felt in a while—that charge, that sense of being seen in a way that made me feel electric. And damn, if it didn't make me stand a little taller, my pulse kicking up at the way he stared at me as though I was everything.

He leaned forward, and my eyes caught on his lips. They were soft and plump, and I wanted a taste. His tongue darted out to wet them, and something about the simple movement sent a strange tension humming through the air. It had been too long. My entire life was hidden by lies, and was it wrong to want something real for myself in this moment?

Yes, it's wrong. Keep your secrets, Brody Vance.

"How's your sugar level?"

He touched the watch on his wrist. "All back to normal." Then, he frowned. "Or as normal as it can be." He laughed then, not fazed by what he'd told me.

"So," I said, breaking the silence, my gaze flicking to the pride pin still attached to his jacket. "You're an ally? The pin, I mean?"

Noah tilted his chin up, meeting my eyes with a quiet defiance that took me off guard. "I'm bi," he said, his tone daring me to say anything about it.

"Cool," I said, keeping my tone neutral, even though the way he held himself—proud, unyielding—made me want to look a little closer. "So, that means you're not a *professional* hockey player?"

"Not yet," he said with a faint smile. "I'm heading to training camp for the Harrisburg Railers. That was the team my dads played for."

"Impressive," I said, leaning back, studying him. "And being queer doesn't... affect your career?"

If he thought that was an odd question, he didn't comment. Instead, his smile softened, but his eyes stayed steady, unwavering. "My dad and pops got married years ago. They paved the way. Some people don't like it, and maybe I won't make the team because of it. Who knows?" He shrugged as if it didn't matter, though the edge in his voice said it did. "But I won't stop being me."

Something about the way he said it, the absolute certainty, made my chest tighten. He didn't apologize for who he was, or flinch, or hide.

I wasn't sure if I admired him or envied him for that. Maybe both.

"Well," I said, unsure of what else to add. "Good for you." His confidence and the quiet defiance in how he carried himself were magnetic, and it took me by surprise. He was the person I'd avoided for too long—steady, self-assured, and unapologetic. My gaze drifted to his curls, golden and wild, and I couldn't help but picture sinking my fingers into them, holding on, anchoring myself to him in a way I hadn't allowed myself to want in years.

"So what was it like dating Jemima Wren?"

"Fuck you," I snapped, and his eyes widened. "Sorry," I added.

"My bad."

I'd only ever been with women. And motorsport wasn't an environment that welcomed anything outside of straight white males. But this man? He tempted me in a way that sent my head spinning. I glanced down at the champagne glass in my hand—it was extra to the whiskey I'd already drunk, which blurred the edges and made all the wildest things possible.

And right now, I was buzzing with something far more potent than alcohol.

Where had the lust come from?

Memories crept in, unbidden, of other times when I'd watched men from the corner of my eye and wondered if one of them could be strong enough to quiet the chaos in my head. To stop me from thinking. To take over and let me breathe, just for a moment.

Not that Noah was strong enough or big enough for that. He wasn't my type. He wasn't...

Why the hell was I even thinking this?

"Are you okay?" Noah asked, his voice uncertain.

Something in me snapped. I'd been asked that question too many damn times lately—by doctors, by Logan, by everyone who thought they had the right to poke at my pain.

"Yes, I'm fucking okay!" I barked, my voice sharper than I intended.

Noah flinched, his eyes widening and a pang of guilt twisted in my chest.

"Sorry," he said, glancing away, but his apology only grated on my nerves.

I didn't want his sorry. I didn't want anyone's pity or cautious words. What I wanted was him—his quiet confidence and the warmth he radiated that made me feel I wasn't sinking for the first time in forever.

My eyes drifted to his lips again, slightly parted, and a bolt of desire shot through me. I shifted in the chair, widening my legs as I leaned back, letting the tension roll off me as best I could. *I'm crazy. Is this the aneurysm making me want things I've never let myself have here?*

"Come here," I said, my voice low, the words more a command than a request.

Noah blinked at me, startled, his breath catching in his throat. And for the first time all night, I felt alive.

Make me feel alive.

FOUR

Noah

OKAY, SO I WAS OFFICIALLY IN THE LAND OF MIXED Messages.

Brody Vance—the king of Formula One sexiness and Jemima *freaking* Wren's ex—was five feet from me, sending off all kinds of mixed vibes. I wasn't sure what I was picking up on my gaydar. On the one hand, he was curt as fuck about my being bi, somewhat accepting but super reserved. On the other, his pretty gray eyes kept going to my mouth, which was so not what a straight guy did.

"Noah," he called my name with a rough purr that made my dick twitch. "Are you involved with someone?"

"Hockey," I stammered, my gaze locked with his. He had a powerful aura that tempted me to me want to forget that five hundred people—two of whom were my fathers —were on the other side of that door. One corner of his mouth drew up. "I mean…"

"No, I know what you mean." He held up a hand and twisted it to show a tattoo of a stylized bird on his wrist. I didn't recognize it, but I guessed it was connected to his racing. "Our sports are our lovers, right? We dedicate our lives to them, and then, out of the blue, they dump us as if we don't matter."

Oh-kay. So, the guy had some baggage with an ex by the sounds. Or was he talking about his sudden hiatus from racing?

"Look, I should maybe just finish up here with my sugar and return to the fundraiser," I said, even as I moved closer to him. He was so fucking cocky, sitting in that armchair like Pacino in *Scarface*, oozing confidence and masculinity.

"Why don't you tend to your medical needs first? Then, we can leave. Do you have a hotel room nearby?"

"Y-yes," I stammered, my grip on my supplies tightening as he nodded, just once, then rose from his seat. I held my ground as he neared, the heady smell of his musky aftershave scrambling my already frazzled brain cells. He got close. His chest and mine were a breath apart, and then, he slid the fingers of his left hand into my hair.

"We should go." His grip tightened a fraction. My cock swelled despite the sounds of laughter and music ten feet away. I wet my lips. His pupils swallowed all that stormy gray with black.

It had been a long time since I'd been with anyone. Who had time? I was working hard to make sure I made the team. Training camp kicked off the next day. I'd shown myself as an asset in development camp and rookie competitions. I'd won a high percentage of my faceoffs at the rookie tournament a few weeks ago—one of my best skills—and scored four goals. That performance had gotten me invited to the *big* training camp. I was not going to blow it. I should be heading home to sleep so that I was in good shape for day one of the most important three weeks of my career. Yet, I was already trying to devise an excuse for the parental units to cut out early.

"I think so, yeah," I replied with a shaky breath.

His mouth met mine then, the tug on my hair pulling me that half an inch required to be tight to him. It was a tentative press of lips to lips. He seemed unsure now, the kiss breaking off as he pulled back a little. Uncertainty flared to life in his gaze.

"I need you to be sure," he whispered, cupping my cheek to caress the new whiskers as if he'd never felt stubble. "*I* need to be sure."

Reeling a bit, I moved in for another kiss to make sure as he insisted. Pops always said that you never got to Graceland if you didn't drive your pink Cadillac with bravado. Which was Pops-speak for being shy never got a man on the team. You had to be forward, self-assured, and know what you wanted. Brody stiffened when my tongue traced the seam of his lips, but then, he not only accepted my tease, he devoured it.

He swept into my mouth, his fingers tightening more on my hair as he probed every molar I possessed, his taste was whiskey and heat and sex. I grabbed his jacket, tugging him into me, and he tugged my hair firmly. A sound I didn't know I could make filled my chest. Not exactly a growl. Not quite a mewl. It was a whimper of pleasure. He moaned gruffly. I released his tux to grab his hips so I could get some friction. He was hard and thick. I met his kiss with a fire I'd never experienced before, and

I'd been with some incredibly hot people. Rachel was a gorgeous girl. Pike, one of the guys on my college hockey team, and I had hooked up whenever the mood had struck, and he was fucking stunning. And while I'd been turned on by both of them, it was nothing in comparison to what feeling Brody's stiff dick rubbing against mine felt like.

"Fuck," I gasped when we broke for air. He held me in place, his fingers tight in my curls, to stare into my eyes as if plumbing my soul for answers to some universal questions. I had no answers. Shit, I didn't know my name right now. All I could think about was the hair-trigger I was working to keep from going off. "So what are we doing here?"

Someone had to ask. If we were going to get into some hot frottage, something I was down for, as I loved some steamy frot, somebody here was going to have to lock the door or make a move for the fire exit.

"Your hotel," he said. I nodded. He rubbed his cheek against mine, murmuring something that sounded like "I never knew," which was confusing as hell.

Never knew what?

Then, he kissed me again. Slower this time, with a tender touch, his mouth less punishing, his hold on my hair lessening. With his mouth on mine, all sensibility left me. I wiggled a hand between us to palm his cock. Brody came unglued. The sweet little kiss turned into a ravenous exploration of my mouth. We pawed at each other as he steered us expertly—as a race car driver would—against the door. The same door that was the only barrier between us and a slew of rich people doing the hustle. He had his dick and mine freed from our pants before I could catch my breath. Not that I wanted to breathe. Oxygen was overrated. Right now, all I needed was Brody Vance. He fumbled with our dicks. I slapped his hand aside. He pulled my head back, his fingers once more fisting my hair.

"Let me," I panted as I got our cocks lined up.

He placed his mouth on my throat, inhaled, and then, licked a wet stripe up my neck. His prick was leaking all over, as was mine. I rocked into my fist, my cock gliding up and down beside his. Brody made low, animalistic sounds against my jugular that ratcheted my need to blow a nut up several thousand increments.

"Shit... I... close," I ground out.

He bucked into my hand, coating my fingers with hot cum. That did it for me. My balls tightened as that white-hot flare at the base of my spine gave me a millisecond of warning before I was spurting as well. He bit down on my throat, the soft burn of his teeth scrubbing my neck, adding to the explosive orgasm. My knees wanted to fold, but I pressed my ass against the door while we both fucked my fist like rabbits. The smell of sex clouded my mind, as did the pulse of our cocks. I twisted free of his hold to find his mouth. Brody kissed me back with wild abandon. His tongue twisting around mine, his hold on my head possessive, perfect. I lapped at his mouth wantonly.

The shrill sound of microphone feedback filled the venue, slicing through the fog of lust we were still bumbling around in.

"Christ," Brody coughed, stepping back, my hold on his lapel keeping him close. "Christ," he said again, stumbling away.

I released his jacket. His eyes were wide, and he spun from me to tuck and zip.

"Uhm…" I said as I felt cool air on my sticky dick. Blushing hotly, I stuffed my spent cock back into my briefs, zipped, and let my shoulder blades rest on the door. I fished out the pocket square Pops had given me to wipe my hand on. "You good?"

"Not in the least," he replied roughly, his shoulders tight, his head hanging low. "That was not good. Not good at all." He turned to face me.

I shoved the dirty hanky back into my pocket. Well, shit. I'd seen that expression of utter devastation once before. Back in high school. Big keg party at some cheerleader's house when her parents were away. One of the football players had been stupidly drunk. Guess he was feeling his bi self once the alcohol hit because he had pulled me into a guest bathroom where I'd given him a sloppy blowjob. I'd been drunk, too, something I rarely did because it fucked with my numbers so bad. But yeah, I'd been tipsy. That dude, Phil, his name had been, acted like Brody did now after he'd shot down my throat. That horrified expression screaming this was a dude who thought he was super straight but had just gotten off with a guy.

"I'm not gay."

Yep, there it was. Shit. Shit. Double shit with a shitty cherry on top. "I'm not either. I'm bi." If I had a dollar for every time I had to clarify…

"That was… I'm not into men," he maintained as his gaze darted to the door. If I hadn't been leaning on it, he would have bolted by now.

"Right. Well, you seemed to be pretty into me when you were fucking my fist, but hey, whatever lie you need to tell yourself is fine."

He gaped as if I'd slapped him. "Fuck you."

"Nice, really nice." I did not need this shit from this guy. Or any guy. If he had been cool about it, then, fine; I get it, it's a lot. But to get rabid? Nope. I moved away from the door, then opened it. His eyes flared. I didn't say a word, I waited, my hand on the antique brass knob.

I could see him chewing on something. If it was an apology, he could keep it. If it was a confession of how he was beyond confused about how good his dick felt next to mine, then cool. The door was open. I could close it. We could talk. It wasn't easy to be out. I got it.

"That stays between us," he snarled as he raked a hand through his hair, then stormed out of the lounge.

"Oh, trust me, asshole, I have *no* plans to tell anyone what a gigantic moron I am for thinking you were hot and cool." I slammed the door shut. Hopefully, it hit his uptight ass. Drawing a shaky breath, I stared at the oil painting above the fireplace. Some dour old man with tiny glasses resting on his nose stared down at me. "Don't even say it," I barked at the portrait as shame coursed through me. I flopped onto a settee, checked my sugar, frowned at the results, and ate a couple of Skittles to steady my fluctuating numbers.

I hadn't counted on the physicality of sex.

I sat there for about ten minutes, working on erasing the last half hour from my memory banks. Yeah, there was no eraser big enough to erase Brody Vance from my head.

Maybe I needed a scrub brush and some bleach…

THE ONLY GOOD THING ABOUT THE FIRST DAY OF TRAINING camp was that I was too busy to wallow about last night's hookup with Brody.

We'd been put through rigorous medical evaluations and physical testing. Nothing quite occupied my mind like aerobic skates, bench press, broad jump, and vertical jump tests. Those joys had been followed by a catered lunch at the new Railers training facility in Carlisle. Sadly, even though the state-of-the-art rink was right across the street from a Dairy Queen, we were discouraged from sneaking over to gorge on ice cream. The lunch was delicious and healthy, with tons of chicken, pasta, some salmon and rice dishes, veggie soup, fruits, and vegetables. My special dietary needs were taken seriously, so I could enjoy a great meal with the guys, a crucial part of starting the bonding process. I sat with some vets who were happy to chat with me to catch up on what my dads were doing now. A couple of younger players joined us, and Brody crept into my thoughts from time to time, but I shoved him back into the dark closet he was hiding in, for now.

There was too much to focus on to let some sexy-as-hell racer with his head stuck in clouds of denial mess with me. I checked my sugar after lunch, was pleased, and stopped super-quick on the way to my first team scrimmage to visit with the team dietician. Steve Figg was a nice guy, youngish, and into ensuring that I ate well. Not that I didn't all the time, but Steve was dedicated to me and my diet. Which I thanked him for repeatedly. I was still tempted to sneak across the road. The siren song of a thick milkshake was loud.

I didn't, though. I geared up, taking a moment to stand in the locker room with all kinds of chaos erupting around me, staring down at the Railers sweater I wore. It was a dark gray one, for offensive players during scrimmages, but it was still an official jersey. I snuck a photo of myself in it, then sent it to my sibs, Pops and Dad, and Rachel. My ex hit me with a GIF with a kitten wearing headphones saying I rocked. My fathers were elated. They could have come down to watch, but they didn't want to steal any of the attention from the press. It was my day, or so they said, and so they stayed home. It killed them, but they did. My sisters all sent wordy replies I would answer later. The team was hitting the ice. I'd been warned that Coach Morin did not tolerate tardiness, so I was out there with the rest of the team and ready for my first practice.

The training facility wasn't the East River Arena by any stretch of the imagination, but it felt like it when I skated up to face off against Jack O'Leary, the oldest player on the team at thirty-seven. He'd played for several teams in his long career but was now looking to retire from the Railers when his contract expired in two years.

"Pay attention, rookie," he teased as Joe Bains, the associate coach, dropped the puck to start a light game between grays and blues.

"You pay attention, sir," I countered, then pounced on the puck as soon as it hit the ice.

I sent it zipping to one of the two wingers I'd been paired with. Nikolai Petrov was a year older than me, a quick little Russian with a crazy one-timer shot. On my other wing was Mason Blake, a sturdy winger who'd been with the Railers for four years. Nikolai rocketed down the ice, Blake and me on his heels, to take a blistering shot on the blue goalie, Lukas Reinhardt. Lukas got his shoulder up to block the shot. The puck fell to the ice in front of the goalie. I dove at it, stick out, and poke-checked it between Reinhardt's legs into the net.

"Good poking!" Nikolai bellowed as he gave me a hand up.

The rest of my line congratulated me–helmet pats, back slaps, and compliments–on giving it my all. Everything was loosey-goosey, giving the zebras on the ice with us little to do. That would change as the scrimmages intensified.

On my way back to the bench for some water, Old Man O'Leary, as the vets called him, skated up to me. He put a big, gloved hand on my shoulder.

"Guess I have someone gunning for my job," he joked while giving my shoulder a pat.

"Maybe, sir," I replied with a smile that made the vet chuckle.

"You can drop that *sir* shit," he huffed in mock offense.

"Okay, ma'am."

The rest of my line howled. Even a few coaches snickered.

Jack palmed my face playfully, then skated off, shouting to the other players that we had a hot shot in the ranks.

I wasn't sure how hot I was, given the guy I'd shared a steaming make-out slash hand-job session with had run from the room as though he'd been sucking face with Nosferatu—the old 1920's vamp, not the newer ones.

Crap. There was Brody again, sneaking into my thoughts. Guess I needed to hockey harder to keep him out of my head. O'Leary and I had the whole afternoon to square off. Surely, that would be enough to drive the racer out of my head for good.

FIVE

Brody

I woke with a pounding headache—not the aneurysm kind, thank God, but the garden-variety hangover kind. Still, it wasn't the best start to the day.

Last night was a blur of sensations I couldn't shake, no matter how hard I tried. Noah had been... unexpected. Everything about him—the way he moved, the sounds he made, the softness of his lips—was seared into my memory like a brand.

The kiss had been electric, his mouth warm and eager, tasting of champagne and something sweeter. When I'd tunneled my hands into his curls, it was like finding the anchor I didn't know I'd been searching for. His hair was as thick and silky as I'd imagined, and the way his breath hitched when my fingers tightened... God, it had been perfect.

I could still hear the sounds he made, quiet gasps breaking free as if he couldn't hold them back, each one more intoxicating than the last. I know it was lust, but in those moments, it felt as if the rest of the world had disappeared.

For a few stolen minutes, everything was simple. Everything made sense. And I couldn't stop replaying it, craving it, even as I tried to tell myself it had been a mistake.

But shit, what the hell had I been thinking?

At least staying at Logan's place was a small comfort. I didn't have to hide here. I could freak out, spiral, and know he'd pull me out of it as he always did. And maybe I could have some Avery time because that little girl and I had fun with the capital F.

Dragging myself out of bed, I pulled on sweats and a T-shirt and followed the faint sounds of clattering to the kitchen. Logan had his head under the sink, tools scattered around him, muttering something about a gasket.

"Where are the girls?" I asked, crouching down beside him.

"Sadie took Avery to the park," he said without looking up. "No one wants to witness me trying my hand at plumbing."

I smirked. "Why don't you just call a plumber? Doesn't my thirty percent cover a plumber?" I'd wanted to give him fifty; he'd been horrified, but what was mine was his—end of story.

Logan chuckled and returned to work, but something about the easy banter didn't sit right. The headache, the regrets—they weren't going anywhere.

"While the girls are out, can we talk?" I said, my voice quieter than I intended.

Logan scooted out from under the sink, his brows

furrowing as he scanned my face. "What's wrong? Is it your head? Do I need to call 911?"

"No, Jesus, Logan." I waved him off, already feeling the tension rising. "I just… I need to talk. I'll make coffee. Meet me in the sunroom in ten."

He watched me for a moment longer, his worry palpable, before nodding. "Okay. Sunroom."

I busied myself with the coffee, the rhythmic motions grounding me just enough to keep the panic at bay. By the time Logan joined me, I was sitting cross-legged on the couch, fiddling with Avery's Lego scattered on the floor.

Logan ambled in, promptly stepping on a piece. "Son of a—" He bit off a curse, glared at the offending item as if he could kill it with his eyes, and sat down, grabbing a mug from the table. "All right, what's up?"

"I kissed a man." I began, not going into full details.

"And you liked it?" Logan sing-songed, then stopped when he saw I was serious.

I hesitated; the words tangled in my throat. Finally, I started recounting the events of the fundraiser—the lounge, the dimly lit room, the voice from the shadows. "His name's Noah," I said. "And he plays hockey. In Harrisburg."

Logan raised an eyebrow, already pulling out his phone. He tapped a few buttons, scrolling through something until he found what he sought. "Hockey player. Harrisburg Railers. Noah Lyamin-Gunnerson. Wow, he's a type 1 diabetic. Guess that's why he was there last night." He turned the phone to a picture, and I nodded, swallowing hard as a picture of Noah's wide, sparkling eyes and easy smile hit me again.

"I'm straight," I blurted, running a hand through my hair.

Logan snorted. "Well, clearly you're not."

I huffed and crossed my arms over my chest. "Well, I'm *supposed* to be straight!"

Logan raised a single eyebrow and sipped his coffee as if he wasn't witnessing me losing my shit. "Who told you that?"

"F1 isn't ready for a queer driver," I snapped.

Again, with the eyebrow thing from my brother. "Who. Told. You. That." he said with exaggerated patience.

"Everyone! The media, the teams, the sponsors... shit, everyone, Lo."

He waited for a beat and sighed again. "Our grandfather?"

"It's a man's sport," I whispered and closed my eyes when Logan nodded sadly. "He always said... and I always... I've had girls–models and actresses–on my arm. I mean Grandfather loved Jemima, said it was the perfect match, and..."

"And?"

"I've never even thought about guys like that." I glanced up at Logan who raised an eyebrow once more. "Shit, that's not true. I've looked before, and I've..." I bunched my hands into fists. "I've wanted, but I've never..."

"But this Noah guy?" Logan prompted.

"I was drunk; I was miserable; I was overwhelmed; and he was kind. He smiled at me, and he has these long curls, and these beautiful, all-knowing eyes, and he made me feel..." I wasn't sure how to finish the sentence.

Logan studied me before setting his mug on the table. "Happy?"

I didn't have an answer. I didn't know if I'd ever have one. All I knew was that Noah had ignited something in me that I couldn't ignore. Something that scared the hell out of me—and made me feel alive.

"Yeah," I said miserably. "For a little while, I was happy."

Logan counted off his fingers. "One, you are a *former* driver; two, Grandfather is a bigoted racist, sexist asshole; and three, what's stopping you when one and two are taken out of the equation?"

Three-year-old Avery launched herself onto my lap with enthusiasm. Her eyes were bright, and she grinned at me. Her tiny hands grabbed my sweater to steady herself.

"I hadta'hav two Skittles, Uncle Brody!" she announced, her voice full of excitement.

"Wow," I said, smoothing her hair and settling her against me.

She beamed; her excitement infectious. "But I'm okay, and I went on the swings! And there were ducks!" she continued, her words tumbling out so fast I couldn't keep up. She leaned against my chest, her small hand waving as she tried to mimic the ducks swimming. I loved holding her like this, feeling her tiny frame against mine, her chatter filling the room.

I caught Logan watching us as Avery rambled about the park and the ducks. He smiled, his expression searching.

"What?" I asked, narrowing my eyes at him.

Logan leaned back in his chair, folding his arms across his chest. "What's stopping you?"

My stomach twisted, his question hitting too close to home. I looked away, focusing on Avery as she chatted about the colors of the ducks' feathers. She didn't have a care in the world, warm and trusting in my arms. And God, I loved this family—Logan, Sadie, and Avery. They were my safe place, the only thing that felt real when everything else spun out of control.

But Logan's words stuck with me, echoing in my head long after the conversation shifted back to Avery and her Skittles.

What *was* stopping me?

I never told Logan I was visiting our grandfather.

Not that he would have stopped me, but I'd have to listen to ten minutes of him cursing about me stepping into the lion's den.

Given my aneurysm was small, stable, and not causing symptoms like dizziness, seizures, or vision problems, the doctor had cleared me to drive, and I always kept one of my cars in Logan's garage.

Thank fuck for that.

He didn't need to drive me anywhere, which meant that when I said I was leaving for home, I could go wherever I wanted.

Including the big old house where my grandfather lived.

I don't know why I answered the summons—but he'd

found out I was in Washington and expected a visit. I thought he'd given up on me. After all, I'd already had speeches ranging from emotional to deranged about giving up racing, and our grandfather was one of those on the list of people I hadn't told about the aneurysm. I fed him the lie of retirement, and he hated it.

I'd spent my entire life carrying the weight of the Vance name in motorsport like a badge of honor—and a noose around my neck. Admitting to the aneurysm? That would be like admitting defeat, like proving him right all along. Weak. A coward. The words he'd never said outright but had always been there, hanging between us, unspoken but sharp enough to cut.

He wouldn't see the aneurysm for what it was—a goddamn ticking time bomb in my skull. No, he'd see it as an excuse, a way to explain why I wasn't good enough. Another reason to question my worth was to remind me that I was failing the family name.

Weakness wasn't tolerated.

And worse, I knew how much he thrived on control. If I told him, it wouldn't end there. He'd take that vulnerability, twist it, use it against me. I'd spent years trying to prove I didn't need him, that I could stand on my own two feet, and telling him the truth would feel like handing him all the power I'd fought so hard to take back.

I hated that I was standing in this house, surrounded by walls that hadn't changed in two decades, feeling like a kid again, crying in my grandmother's arms after everything had fallen apart.

I stopped outside my grandfather's office and paused,

staring at a photo that had hung there for as long as I could remember.

The three Vance kids—Logan was twelve, me nine, and Charlie, only seven. We all looked so much alike, with our mom's dark hair and our dad's pale gray eyes. It had been taken a few weeks before the accident—Mom, Dad, and Charlie—gone in an instant. A plane crash—Dad piloting, probably drunk—that shattered everything we knew. After that, it was just Logan and me, two grieving kids trying to navigate a new world. Of course, we had family; our grandparents took us in, but living with our grandfather became both a blessing and a curse. He was a racer like me, more of a legend in motorsport than I could ever be, and he poured everything he knew into us. We had every advantage to reach the pinnacle of racing: the best trainers, the best karts, the sponsors, and the legacy of what our grandfather–and to a lesser extent, my father–had achieved.

Everyone knew *one* of the Vance boys *had* to drive.

It was an inescapable destiny.

But then, Logan turned his back on racing, paid his own way through college, and met Sadie. Grandfather had never spoken to Logan with anything less than open hostility after that. It infuriated Grandfather that Logan was my manager and handled contracts for several other high-profile athletes. He'd become a success on his own terms.

Shoulders back, jaw tight, I knocked once—sharp, purposeful—and then, opened the door without waiting for him to shout about me wasting his time loitering outside. Because he would've, and we both knew it.

"Sit," he barked as soon as I stepped into the room, his tone cutting.

I swallowed the lump in my throat, schooling my features into the calm, detached mask I'd perfected over the years. I sat slowly, my back stiff, my jaw tight, waiting for whatever storm he was about to unleash.

His office was a shrine to his eighties glory days, a museum of the man he still believed himself to be. Photos lined the walls—him grinning with a champagne bottle in hand, standing next to his world championship-winning car, girls in tiny outfits kissing his cheeks—none of them my grandmother. Helmets were displayed on a shelf–pristine and untouched by time–and a massive cabinet gleamed with trophies he'd collected over his career.

And in the center of it all, behind a vast oak desk that seemed to fill the room, was the man I loved and hated equally.

At seventy-five, he was still strong, his presence as dominating as ever. His gray hair was neatly combed, his face lined but sharp, his pale eyes—still piercing. In this room, he wasn't just my grandfather. He was the king of an empire he'd built from nothing, off the back of an engineering degree and a racing career that had made him a household name.

I respected him for what he'd done. For racing in an era when cars were little more than death traps, on tracks with unsafe barriers, in a sport where death wasn't only a risk—it was an inevitability. He'd seen, survived, and built something legendary from it.

But I also hated that he was stuck in that time when he was my age and had the world at his feet. He wore his glory as armor, clinging to it so tightly it had become his identity. And God help anyone who didn't live up to the standard he'd set for himself back then.

I respected the man, but my irrational temper was already flaring, and he hadn't opened his mouth yet.

He leaned forward in his chair. "Okay, enough is enough, Brody." His voice rose, and he slammed a hand on the desk, echoing through the room. "I have sponsors contacting me, asking what's going on. I have journalists calling every hour, digging for answers. I've lost contracts because of you. Do you have any idea how this makes me look? After everything I've done for you?"

Wow, not even a hello. I opened my mouth, but he didn't give me a chance to respond.

I flinched despite myself, hating how he could still make me feel small, as if I were nine years old and being scolded for scuffing my new kart. He had this way of distilling pure contempt into his words, hard and cold, and hurling them right where they would hurt the most.

"Grandfather, I retired—"

"Enough!" His eyes narrowed, drilling into mine, and his voice dropped, colder now, sharper. "What are you? Afraid? Is that it? Are you too much of a coward to get back in the car? Too weak to face the pressure? To face the legacy I handed you on a silver platter?"

My head snapped up at that, the words hitting me like a punch to the gut.

My throat tightened, his words hitting every raw nerve I had left. *Coward. Weak.* Words from him I'd spent my entire life trying to outrun, words I'd built my career to silence. And now, he was dragging them out into the open, daring me to deny them.

But what could I say?

Tell him the truth.

"You owe me, Brody. Do you understand that? You wouldn't be where you are if it weren't for me. Every victory you've had, every podium and contract comes back to me."

Tell him.

The words were stuck in my throat. I didn't want his pity. I didn't want him to coddle me like a broken toy or, worse, weaponize my condition in whatever power game we were always playing. I'd be damned if I'd let him turn it into another reason to control me.

"I'm not going back."

"You're the same as Logan," he spat, his face flushed. "Ungrateful, selfish, weak. I gave you everything, and this is how you repay me. By ruining everything I've worked for? Everything our name stands for?"

My heart pounded, and his words reverberated in my skull. I stared at him, the man who had dominated my entire life, who had been both a mentor and a jailer. My grandfather had been a master of discipline, believing every mistake was an opportunity to be better—sharper, faster, more focused. He'd drilled that into me from the moment I first sat in a kart, calm but relentless, pointing out every flaw, every misstep, every tiny detail.

Focus, Brody. Again. Do it again until it's perfect.

And I had. Over and over. I wanted to make him proud, and I scrambled for every approval, which rarely came. It made me a strong driver—a better one. I couldn't deny that. The focus and the ability to block out everything except the track in front of me came from him.

But it had destroyed parts of me too.

Every time I fell short, every time I wasn't perfect, it felt as if I wasn't just failing him—I was failing myself. That constant need to prove I was good enough, fast enough, smart enough had carved something raw and unrelenting into my chest, a wound that never quite healed.

I learned how to handle and thrive under pressure, but I also learned how to tear myself apart when I didn't live up to it. He never yelled or raised a hand, but his silence when I messed up was worse than any punishment.

And now, years later, I could still hear him in the back of my mind whenever I faltered. *"Focus, Brody. Again."*

It had made me a champion. But at what cost?

"Right, I've decided what's happening. I'll allow you to take this year as a sabbatical," Grandfather said, his tone leaving no room for argument. Not that it mattered—he always talked as if his word was law. "Get back to training Because, look at you, you're soft. Your neck muscles are diminished, and have you put on weight?"

I clenched my jaw, my hands curling into fists at my sides. "Only a couple of—"

"Then, get back with that woman. The singer. She's doing okay, and you could use the good publicity."

"Jemima? No, I—"

"We'll announce you're coming out of retirement," he continued, leaning back in his chair with confidence. "Something about rediscovering your passion, some... woke thing about finding yourself. People eat up that kind of nonsense these days. It'll be perfect. And then, we'll get you back, and this time, you won't fuck up and miss the championship by twenty-three Goddamn points!"

He spoke as if it were a done deal.

It took everything in me not to snap, not to stand up and yell that soft didn't mean shit when you were fighting to stay alive. That no amount of training could fix a goddamn aneurysm in your brain. But I stayed silent.

Because what was the point? He'd already decided. And in his world, what he decided was reality. Whether I liked it or not.

I stared at him. I didn't have an answer.

And then, I stood.

I didn't say a word. I didn't yell, didn't argue, didn't explain myself. I just turned on my heel and walked out of the room, his voice following me down the hall.

"Don't you dare walk away from me, Brody! You hear me? Don't you dare!"

But I didn't stop. I didn't look back. Because, for once, I wouldn't give him the satisfaction.

"We're not done! I know where you'll be."

He expected me to go to the house on Lake Michigan, my apartment in Monaco. Or maybe that I'd stay with Logan, Sadie, and Avery.

"Well fuck you, old man," I snapped.

I peeled out of the gates in my Maserati, heading for the open road, and drove north to find somewhere else to hide.

Harrisburg.

SIX

Noah

I'D BEEN COMING IN AROUND THE BACK OF THE NET, DOING my best to try to sneak the puck past Dmitry, but he was too fast. One big skate came out to rest on the post, blocking the wrap-around attempt. Dmitry, then, fell on the puck, freezing it, and one of the refs blew the puck dead as the players on my gray team circled the net like sharks.

"Nice try, rookie," the Russian called from behind his mask. The Railers emblems on his shiny mask reminded me I wasn't dreaming. I was really here working my ass off trying to make the team. "Has your papa not told you that there is no slipping pucks on the sly past Russian goalies?"

He tossed the puck to a ref.

"He might have, but I figured you might be super tired from all the shots on goal we grays have been taking."

That made the good-looking goalie laugh. "You worry over your tired. My tired is not so very tired," he replied, his thick accent similar to my pops. "If you are not too sleepy after this, many few of us are going to race after lunch. Come with us. Then, I can block you in go-karts as well as on ice."

"Sounds good," I said, giving him a gloved hand to catcher bump, then skated to the bench. Coach Morin was watching me closely. Not just me, obviously, but all of us. Still, I felt as if his attention was locked on me as I took a seat between my wingers. I glanced at Blake, scrubbing his face with a towel. "You going to the go-kart thing after practice?"

"Yeah, it's fun. And Coach suggested it as a bonding thing. You going?"

"I guess. I mean I feel like I should maybe spend more time on the ice. My speed sprints weren't as good as I would have liked…"

"Gunny, seriously, your speed sprints blew ninety percent of us away." I kind of liked how, after only one day, I had my official nickname. That made me feel as if I were part of the team, even though I could be sent down at any moment. "Coach said we should go, so go. You can sleep here on the bench tonight to make sure you're here when they unlock the doors at six."

I blushed. Okay, so yeah, I'd been here at six this morning to put in extra ice time before the rest of the guys arrived. Coach had arrived first, picking me out on the ice practicing one-timers. He'd not said anything—he wasn't a big talker unless you fucked up, then he talked right into your face–but he took note. Dedication. That was what got you on the final roster.

Going the extra mile. Pushing harder than the other

rookies. That would secure my spot. Not standing on the ice alone shooting pucks at the net while my mind drifted to the sounds Brody Vance had made when he came. Which was why the sound of frozen rubber hitting glass was so prevalent during my solo time. The man was in my head. No matter what I did, I couldn't shake him. Maybe an afternoon out with some of the Railers was what I needed. Just some fun. Simple, easy guy stuff.

"I would like to race against you as well," Nikolai added after rinsing the lactic acid from his mouth, then spitting the rinse water into the air in an arc that almost hit one of the linesmen. "I see that maybe you drive like you check. Only little bumps in the backside."

"Last I heard, you liked bumps in the backside," Blake tossed out.

Nikolai snickered.

Okay, so the walls were dropping. Seemed at least one of my future teammates—think positive Dad always says —was a little queer?

"I am liking bumps in the backside just fine," Nik replied as he slung his leg over the boards. "You should know this, yes?"

My eyes went wide. No shit, were these two getting it on?

"He's talking shit. We never bumped backsides," Blake said as we hit the ice. "He likes to stir the pot when he can. We went out one time. No sparks, decided to be buddies. I mean, dating your teammate is tricky. If you break up, there's shit in the locker room."

"Yeah, that would suck," I concurred.

"Big time. So you racing?"

"I'll be there." I held out my fist.

Blake thumped it as we skated in for the faceoff. Which I won, handily. Not to brag but... yeah, I was bragging to myself. That was a killer skill to have, and the coaches were keeping track. I'd have to buy my dads an extra tie for Father's Day for all the time spent on the ice honing that talent.

The scrimmage lasted for about forty-five minutes, the blues beating the grays by one goal. I'd done pretty well overall, I felt, so when I got called off the ice by Coach Morin, I went along, as did O'Leary. My nerves spiked a bit. Why was the captain needed in this talk? Shit, was I being sent down already?

"Nothing to worry over," Jack whispered as we *thunked* our way down the cattle chute towards the offices. "Just some medical stuff."

Oh, okay, yeah that tracked. We pushed into the team doctor's office.

The doctor's office felt cramped with everyone crammed inside—Coach Morin in a chair; Steve, team nutritionist extraordinaire, and Jack O'Leary, team captain and a role model of mine, leaning against the wall. We'd been called in for one of *those* meetings... the kind where people dissect my vulnerabilities due to diabetes. But I was used to this kind of scrutiny. It came with the territory, and honestly? I was good at handling it. If I made the team, there would also be a professional available to support me, but of course, that was an added cost to the Railers and might be the one thing that took me off their list. The team athletic trainer, Jordan Mahesh, was here, too, as was the team physician, Dr. John Tibel. I'd talked to the team doc online, but this was the first time we'd met in person. I shook everyone's hands, then sat.

I leaned forward in my chair, trying not to fidget as all their eyes focused on me. I wasn't nervous, but I didn't want to come off as overconfident, either. I wasn't on the team yet.

Steve adjusted his glasses, and his voice was calm and professional as he picked up the iPad, where the data from the continuous glucose monitor I wore was sent. The same information ruled my life—available on my phone and watch.

"Now, we've already talked at length, Noah, but for our records, you're wearing a CGM on your chest during training, and I have the data here that looks good."

"Thank you."

"How has that been working out for you?" Dr. Tibel asked.

"It's been... fine," I said, patting where the disc sat beneath my shirt. "I'm used to a CGM—I've been wearing one for years. Switching to my chest has required some adjustment, but I've managed well. The readings have been quite accurate."

"And you're managing with injections instead of a pump."

"Yeah, a pump would be dangerous. One hit, and it could stop working."

He nodded, tapping a note. "Good call. How's practice been? Any lows?"

I hesitated, glancing at Coach and Cap before answering. "I had a couple of warnings," I admitted. "But I caught potential lows early. I've got gels and tabs on hand,

and I've been careful to check my numbers regularly. I don't want to be a liability out there."

Cap raised an eyebrow, his arms crossed. "You're not a liability, but if you're on the ice and something happens, it affects the whole team."

"Yeah, I know," I said quickly, not wanting to sound defensive. "I've been managing diabetes for years. I've established routines. I understand my body, and I know how to handle it."

Steve nodded. "Consistency is key—checking your levels before, during, and after practice, and ensuring you're fueling properly."

Cap's smirk softened into something more encouraging. "You've got potential, rookie. Just focus on what you can control, and the rest will fall into place."

"Thanks," I said, my voice steady, though my heart raced. I wasn't only proving myself to them—I was proving it to myself too. And while I wasn't on the team yet, I knew I could earn that spot. I just had to show them.

When the med meeting was over I rushed to the locker room to shower, change, and meet up with the guys. They'd lingered in the hall, waiting for me, which made me feel pretty good. In a pack of about a dozen players—mostly single guys, as the married players were heading home—we made our way out of the players' exit, waving at one of the security guys as we exited. The weather was warm. Fall wasn't officially here yet, but you could see autumn in the shorter days of September.

We all piled into our cars. I dug inside my personal bag for a snack-size bag of assorted nuts to munch on. Settled behind the steering wheel, I cracked open a bottle of spring water, synced my phone to the stereo, and tore open the little green package of nuts. At the moment "No One Mourns the Wicked" blasted out of the speakers, I caught sight of a fire-red Maserati skidding into the parking lot. Whoever was behind the wheel was either super skilled or stupid ballsy. He slid sideways into a slot by the players' entrance. Ooh, I was impressed. *Not.*

"Dumb ass showoff," I mumbled as Glinda began to sing. Now, I couldn't possibly hit the notes that Ariana did, but I gave it my best as I reversed out of my spot, my head filled with lyrics as I left the arena behind.

Krazy Karts HBG was one of my favorite places to hang out. Having lived in this area my whole life, I knew exactly where to go, so I arrived right behind the rowdy crew known as the Dirty Dozen. We joked around as we entered the indoor racetrack, teasing each other and calling each other out—just that kind of shit. The team had reserved the track for us for two hours of team bonding. Nothing communicates I-want-to-work-hard-alongside-you quite like crashing into your coworkers to cause them to wipe out.

The track was being readied for us, so we lingered in the lobby shooting the shit as guys do. Talk drifted from hockey to women to music. Blake, Nik, and I were standing by the front door beside a vast board with local events pinned to it when the door flew open, sending the pamphlets into a frenzy as a blast of warm air entered with a man in dark shades and a ballcap pulled low on his head. I gave him a quick glance, started to reply to something Blake said, and then, the realization of who was here hit me. It was his mouth. Those lips. I'd kissed those lips only a few days ago.

"Brody?" I choked out. He paused at the door, his gaze swinging my way as those lush lips of his flattened.

"I'm incognito," he snapped, then moved inside, the door gliding shut behind him. We had a moment, and not one of those romantic, drawn-out lovers reunited moments. More like a what-the-fuck-do-I-say-now moment. "I went to the arena, but you'd left."

"Dude, stalker much?" I asked.

My linemates had fallen silent.

"What?! I... no, of course not. Why would... please. No, I was just in the city and wanted to check in to see if you were okay."

My brows knitted, and I moved closer and lowered my voice. "Seriously? What? You think that you're so amazingly stunning that I would be lying in my bed crying into my pillow because we jerked each other off? You're really not all that, Brody Vance."

He *really was* all that. Totally all that and a box of thin mints. Fuck, now I wanted a mint chocolate chip milkshake. Brody was nothing but bad for me.

"Why don't you just announce our shit to the world?!" he snapped.

"Fuck, I—"

"I'm incognito," he said under his breath and took off his glasses. Every hockey player in the waiting lounge gasped. Yeah, after dating Jemima Wren, he was *that* famous. And fuck me, just as gorgeous. "Did I not say that I wasn't—"

"Oh. My. God," someone shouted—thankfully, not one of the team.

Two members of the go-kart staff rushed over to get selfies and autographs.

"Oh hey, how are you?"

I slunk off as Brody did the publicity stuff that he did so well. Smiling, charming everyone in the place, making people feel important when he didn't give two shits about them; otherwise, he wouldn't have been so cold to them when they'd shared an intimate moment. Oh no, wait, it was only me he treated like a cold sore.

"Gunny, you feeling okay?" Blake asked as he and Nikolai joined me in the far corner.

"I'm good, just shocked to see someone I know here," I lied, then felt bad about it.

"You know Brody Vance?" Nik asked, his eyes wide.

"Friend of a friend," I dismissed.

"Mmmm Jemima Wren," Nik added, "driver is big lucky."

"So, how about we sign in for this karting." I tried to move them along, because Brody didn't want anyone to know he was into guys, and I didn't want to do any more lying, so whatever. I'd cover his ass on that front even though I'd whispered some pretty personal crap a few minutes ago. And now I felt guilty. No one should be outed, no matter how bad they made you feel. *Shit. Shit. Shit.* Now, I had to fucking apologize to Brody.

"You two seemed very tense-filled," Nik whispered as he glanced over Blake to glare at Brody. "Is there fiction between you two?"

"Friction, he means friction," Blake explained when I shot Nik a confused glance.

"We just kind of know each other," I lied, again. "Didn't really hit it off. Nothing big." I forced a smile that they accepted, mostly.

When the rush of people wanting to breathe the same air as Brody died down, he made his way to me. The hat now resting on some staff member's head, his sunglasses tucked so debonairly into the *V* of his polo shirt. The dude looked like he'd stepped off the cover of *GQ,* and that irked me to no end. It also made my dick perk up, which irked me even more.

"They said they wouldn't share photos for a while," he said, as if that mattered to us. "And hey, I hope you don't mind me showing up like that." He was talking to me alone, when my linemates pulled a Homer Simpson melting into the bushes. Then, he lowered his voice. "I really wasn't stalking you. I'd just had a rough moment back in… look… I don't know why, but I found myself driving here."

"Cool. Whatever. You do you, man."

"I thought that we could maybe talk after we raced."

Talk. What the—Wait. Racing? "Are you shitting me? *You're* racing? Here? With us?"

"They all want me to." He waved a hand at the rest of the Railers, staring at him as if he were some godhead. "I can see that you're not feeling that so—"

"No, hey, I would love to race you." What kind of jerk would I be to deny the guys the chance to race a Formula One legend? Or, more importantly, to Nik, someone who'd had sex with Jemima Wren. I waited as he processed. He seemed unsure of... well, everything. That uncertainty made him seem a little less asshole and a little more human. Just a little. Like the size of a dust mote.

"Okay. That's fun." He pushed out. The man looked as if he were about to have a dental extraction without any laughing gas. I felt that way too, so we did have that in common.

"Cool. Yeah. Fun."

So very not.

SEVEN

Brody
_____

THE SCENT OF FUEL HIT ME WHEN I STEPPED INTO THE garage, sharp and familiar, tugging me back to the first time I'd ever karted as a kid. I could still remember the hum of the tiny engine, the way every vibration traveled through the frame, right into my body. Back then, it felt like magic—feeling the track through my ass, every bump, every weight shift, as if the kart was alive beneath me.

Now, standing in front of these rental karts, it wasn't quite the same, but it was close enough to spark something in me. The karts were simple machines—two-stroke engines, about 15 horsepower, maybe two hundred pounds, if that. With a good power-to-weight ratio and a flat track, they could hit fifty or sixty miles per hour. It wasn't Formula 1 speeds, but on a tight circuit, that would be fast enough to make it fun.

We put on the rental overalls, which were loose and thin compared to the tight, multilayered suits I was used to. These weren't fireproof high-tech gear plastered in sponsor logos, but I barely noticed the difference, too busy watching Noah across the garage.

He laughed with a tall guy he called Blake. His voice was light and easy, and his curls bounced as he tugged his overalls over his legs. Now and then, his shirt rode up, revealing glimpses of skin—just enough to make my chest tighten and my mind wander.

I couldn't stop thinking about the feel of him, the way he'd melted into me that night as if he'd been waiting for it as much as I had. The kiss had been a battle, both of us fighting for control, for dominance, for something more than either of us was ready to admit.

I yanked the zipper up on my overalls, trying to ignore the way my pulse quickened just watching him, and my cock plumped up—thank god the overalls were loose. This was supposed to be about racing, about losing myself in the track's speed and thrills. But I could only focus on Noah and how he made me feel as though I was hurtling out of control—even when we were standing still.

"All right, Racer Boy," one of the guys said, grinning like he'd already won. "How many laps do we get as a head start?"

"Ten?" someone else said, and the group laughed.

I smirked, walking along the row of karts, my hand trailing over the frames as I examined them. "Ten laps?" I echoed, shaking my head. "What do you think I am, a charity? You get five. No more."

"Five?" the first guy said, crossing his arms. "You drive fast cars for a living, man. Five laps is nothing."

"I did," I corrected, the word slipping out sharper than intended. "I was a F1 driver. Big difference."

That shut him up, and I stepped back, clapping my hands together. "All right, enough whining. Let's get on with it. My face will end up all over social media as soon as we start, and I've got about an hour before everyone figures out where I am."

The guys exchanged glances, excited. Maybe they knew they were about to get smoked, but that was part of the fun.

I climbed into one of the karts, the seat hard and unforgiving but oddly comfortable. With a pull of the cord, the engine roared to life, and the familiar vibrations traveled up through the seat, settling into my bones.

This. This was what I'd missed. The speed, the focus, and its freedom, and I was happy the g-forces here wouldn't be enough to cause an issue. This wasn't F1. It was fun.

Even if my grandfather somehow got wind of this through social media, I'd be long gone before that wily bastard could track me down.

I grinned, adjusting the straps and gripping the wheel. "Five laps, gentlemen. Better make them count."

The others were already out on the track, engines buzzing like angry bees as they tore into their first lap. I waited in the pit, leaning back in the kart, watching the chaos unfold. Blake was trying too hard, his kart fishtailing as he oversteered into the first corner. On the other hand, Noah had settled into a smooth rhythm, his lines tight, his focus unmistakable.

Five laps. That was the deal. They were having fun, whooping, hollering, and laughing so loud it hurt my heart. I missed this.

When they'd completed their fifth lap, I pulled my helmet down and hit the gas. The kart shot forward; the engine roaring as I joined the race.

It didn't take long to find my rhythm. The kart was light and responsive, every bump and curve translating directly into my body. This was pure driving—no high-tech controls, no engineers fine-tuning settings, me, the machine, and the track.

By the time the others hit the middle of lap eight, I was already closing in. The first guy didn't stand a chance. He was wide out of the corner, leaving a gap big enough for me to slip through without trying. One down.

Two more drivers were bunched together, their karts bumping as they jockeyed for position. I waited, letting them make their mistakes. One braked too late, sliding out, and the other got distracted trying to avoid him. I breezed past both of them as if they weren't there.

Noah and Blake were out in front, still holding their lead. I caught up to Blake first. He was fast but couldn't keep it clean, his rear wheels skidding as he fought to stay ahead. I took the inside line on the next corner, cutting him off. He cursed—probably loud enough for me to hear if I hadn't been focused on the next target.

Noah was different. He wasn't just fast; he was smooth. He knew how to hold his line and make himself hard to pass. I stayed close, watching for an opening, and when I pulled alongside him, I glanced over.

He was locked in, his gaze sharp, his hands steady on the wheel. For a second, I almost didn't want to pass him. He looked... incredible. Focused, determined, and entirely in the moment. But then, he glanced at me, and I saw the flicker of surprise in his eyes.

I grinned under my helmet, put my foot down, and left him in my rearview.

The rest of the race was mine. By the time I crossed the finish line, I was half a lap ahead when I slowed to let them catch me. I pulled into the pit, yanking off my helmet as the others rolled behind me.

Noah climbed out of his kart, pulling off his helmet and shaking his curls loose, his face flushed with exertion. He caught my eye, and for a second, it was just the two of us, the noise of the track fading into the background.

I felt fantastic. It wasn't only the win—the speed, simplicity, and pure joy of being behind the wheel again.

"You're insane," Blake laughed, throwing his hands up. "Who even does all that shit out there?"

I shrugged, a cocky grin spreading across my face. "What can I say? I've got skills."

Noah laughed, shaking his head as he walked toward me. "Next time, it's a ten-lap head start."

"Next time?" I asked, my grin widening. "You sure you're ready for more of me?"

God. What was I saying? I didn't mean karting. I meant more of me. More kissing, more of him pressed against me, his hands in my hair, his lips on mine. More getting off against doors, taking it to a bed where we wouldn't have to rush or hold back. Fuck. He was beautiful—his curls damp and wild, his eyes bright with excitement.

Noah stared at me, and it felt as though the rest of the world disappeared for a moment. His lips parted slightly, and I could almost hear the echoes of the sounds he'd made that night. His gaze held mine, steady and searching, and it was as if he could see everything I wasn't saying.

I wanted to kiss him. Right there, in front of everyone. Pull him close, let him feel the pounding of my heart, tell him with my body what my words couldn't quite form.

"Noah—"

A hard slap on my shoulder broke the moment, and I jerked back, my pulse racing.

"Hey, Racer Boy," Blake said with a grin, oblivious to our tension. "Looks like someone shared your location."

I glanced over my shoulder and cursed under my breath. A group of people had gathered outside the glass doors, their phones out, snapping pictures.

"Great," I muttered, running a hand through my hair.

"Better get your celebrity act together," Blake teased.

I sighed, pulling off the overalls and tossing them onto a nearby bench. My neck cracked as I rolled it, the tension easing. Then, I slapped on the smile I'd perfected over the years—the one that left people happy, no matter how fake it felt.

The doors opened, and I stepped into the crowd. It was the usual chaos—shouts of my name, hands thrusting notebooks, photos, and phones at me. I signed everything, even an arm, grinning like I wasn't trying to keep my thoughts from straying back to Noah.

Selfies followed; the fans' excitement contagious as it grated on the part of me that wanted to be me for a few minutes longer. Their voices buzzed around me, questions firing off like rapid-fire bullets, one after another.

"Why did you retire?"

"You were so close to winning!"

"Are you making a comeback?"

"Are you back with Jemima?"

"Is *Jemody* back on-track?"

"Is it true that—"

I tuned them all out, the noise blurring into a dull hum. My smile stayed in place, practiced and automatic, as I posed for another photo, signed another notebook, and nodded to another eager fan. But inside? I was somewhere else.

The truth was, I didn't have answers for them—not the kind they wanted, anyway. Why did I retire? Because my life depended on it. Because I didn't have a choice. But none of them could know that. The polished lie the PR team had spun—about stepping back to explore new opportunities—was what they'd cling to, no matter how fake it sounded.

So, I kept my head down, kept my responses vague, and kept moving. Because letting any of it sink in—letting myself feel the weight of their questions—would've been too much.

I wasn't their Brody Vance anymore. Hell, I wasn't even sure I was mine.

When the crowd thinned, I waved them off with a practiced charm, climbed into my Maserati—gutted I couldn't stay and talk to Noah—and revved the engine.

Through the windshield, I saw Noah and Blake still where I'd left them. Noah was watching me, his expression unreadable, but his eyes stayed locked on mine until I pulled out of the lot.

I left them standing there, my pulse still racing for reasons unrelated to the car's speed.

I woke up in my hotel room to the faint hum of traffic outside, the sunlight streaming through the cheap blinds that didn't quite close all the way. I'd deliberately picked this place—small, in the middle of nowhere, far enough outside Harrisburg that no one would connect the dots. So far, no one had asked questions or looked at me twice.

The first thing I did was check my phone, and I regretted it. The motorsport press had gone wild with its speculation.

Brody Vance Spotted in Pennsylvania—Is He Eyeing a New Team?

Jemima's ex slumming it?

Brody Vance's Mysterious Karting Adventure— Comeback in the Works?

And worse.

Brody Vance: The Driver Who Walked Away—Why Did The Quitter Desert His Team on the Verge of Victory?

Quitter? I wasn't a damn quitter. But that didn't stop some gutter media from painting me as one. Every article and social post dissected my decision as if they had the right to. As if they knew me, as if they understood what I'd been through. They didn't feel the ache in my chest every time I thought about what I'd lost—what I'd been forced to walk away from.

But that didn't matter. To them, I was just another

story. A name that fell from the headlines of glory into the pit of controversy. A driver who'd given up when he was only points away from the championship.

I didn't quit. I survived. And sometimes surviving looks an awful lot like walking away. What if Noah saw this and judged me, and I wouldn't get a chance to show him I wasn't an asshole without telling him the whole story.

I can't tell anyone.

"Fuck this," I told my phone and switched it off.

Now what? I had no plans but to see Noah. I wanted to talk to him, but how did I see him? Should I call? I didn't have his number.

I could find it if I wanted to, or I could see him, talk to him, and exchange numbers naturally as normal people do.

I had to turn my phone back on, ignoring the notifications. Instead, I did some quick searching and found out the Railers team was at their practice facility, with guys like Noah trying to make the cut.

"I'm going there incognito. I'm going to ask him out for coffee. I can apologize some more. We'll have sex, and I *will* get him out of my system and then, I can move on. Decision made."

My coffee maker wasn't impressed by my decision, letting out what sounded like a sigh as the final coffee dripped into the mug.

Outside, ready to leave, I stared at my Maserati. If I wanted to stay low-key, maybe it wasn't about dark glasses and a hat—it was about ditching the car. So now what?

"Nice car," Eddie murmured. He and Joan were an

older couple who ran the hotel, and he'd followed me outside with some packages to post.

"Yeah," I said, and it hit me. "Any chance you've got something I could borrow for the day? A little more... low-key?"

Eddie glanced at me, and I could see his confusion. However, his expression softened when he called Joan out, and I offered them a way-over-the-odds amount to rent their Toyota for the day. Money has a way of smoothing out questions.

Eddie handed me the keys to an ancient silver Corolla, muttering something about "not driving it like one of those race cars." Tall and lanky, he'd been the last to drive it, so I had to adjust the seat to fit my five-nine frame.

"Weird guy," I heard Joan whisper to him as I drove off. But they were satisfied with the money, so that was that.

The drive into Harrisburg was quiet, my phone directing me to the Railers training complex. I still didn't know what the hell I was doing. I wasn't a hockey guy— I'd grown up in motorsport, which had consumed my life. I parked the Corolla in the back of the lot, grateful for how nondescript it was, and made my way inside, keeping my head low. The complex was open to the public, so I didn't have to talk my way past anyone at the entrance, and apart from a bag check—I had nothing—they let me in.

The stands weren't packed, but enough people were scattered around to make it feel as if every eye was on me. I slunk up to the top row and sat down, hoping no one here cared enough about motorsport to notice me.

What was I doing here? I didn't know a thing about

hockey, and from what I could tell, this wasn't a real game. On the ice, the players were scattered, most kneeling as the guy in charge—probably the coach—gestured and barked orders.

I leaned back in my seat, watching the organized chaos unfold below me. Noah was easy to spot, even after he put on his helmet, his sharp movements and focus setting him apart. He looked good out there—damn good.

I felt like an idiot. Cars had consumed my life, and sitting alone in a hockey rink, I was pretending I wasn't here for reasons I couldn't quite admit to myself.

The pitiful excuses I'd prepared sounded better in my head than they did out loud. Still, I told myself I wasn't stalking Noah. I was… curious. Curious enough to know where he trained, when he was on the ice, and—okay, yes—I was a stalking stalker. But hell, I wasn't doing anything nefarious with the information.

Practice shifted into something more intense, the players breaking off into teams—gray shirts against blue. Even from the nosebleeds, I could see the change in pace, the way every pass and play was more deliberate. The rubber disc—puck, I reminded myself—skated across the ice, but my focus was on Noah.

He was the best out there. He moved as if he'd been born to do this. His speed was ridiculous, and I caught glimpses of other players darting across the ice, but they barely registered. Noah commanded my attention, his every movement pulling me in. How he twisted around other skaters trying to stop him, the sharp snap of his wrist sending the puck sailing into the net—amazing.

So, fucking sexy.

My chest tightened as I watched him skate back to the center, his shoulders rising and falling as he caught his breath. He was unstoppable, powerful, and beautiful.

And me? I was sitting in the shadows, trying to convince myself I was here to watch a practice, not to lose myself in how he made me feel like I couldn't look elsewhere.

I turned my phone back on to check something—anything—that would stop me losing my shit and heading out on the ice to talk to him. The only messages I focused on were one from my grandfather insisting I return home, and the other… well, that I could handle—a message from Jemima.

JEMIMA: HEY YOU
   Brody: Hey you, back
   Jemima: You doing okay, sweetheart?

SHE ADDED SEVERAL HEARTS AND KISSES—DEFINITELY ON-brand for the queen of pop.

No, I'm losing my shit, my head hurts, everything is fucked up.

Of course, I didn't send that.

BRODY: I THINK I'M BISEXUAL

WELL, I NEVER EXPECTED TO SEND THAT!

. . .

JEMIMA: *I KNOW YOU ARE*
   Brody: ????
   Jemima: You remember our midnight chats about Davey?

SHIT, YES, I REMEMBERED DAVEY, A ROADIE, HIM OF THE purple hair and the pretty blue eyes and the...
   Shit.
   I'm bisexual for sure.

BRODY: *FUCK*
   Jemima: LOL. It's okay. Are you with someone? Interested in someone? Do you want to call and talk?
   Brody. No, yes, and no, I can't talk right now.

I PAUSED FOR A MOMENT.

BRODY: *IF I COME OUT AS BI, WILL IT CAUSE YOU trouble?*

THERE WAS A PAUSE AT HER END.

. . .

JEMIMA: IF I COME OUT AS POLY, WILL IT CAUSE YOU trouble?

WHAT?

BRODY: OF COURSE NOT
   Jemima: Likewise

I SMILED. SHE WAS SO MATTER-OF-FACT AND DOWN TO earth—if only things had worked out with her, then I wouldn't be facing my existential crisis.

I wouldn't have allowed myself to be attracted to Noah. Or fuck his hand. Or kiss him.

BRODY: I MET A GUY
   Jemima: I met a girl
   Jemima: I have to go. Xxx
   Jemima: Love you B
   Brody: Back at ya J xx

I WAS DRAWN DOWN TO THE PLEXIGLASS SURROUNDING THE training rink, which I assumed was to stop random pucks from hitting viewers. I couldn't help myself. It wasn't rational, and it wasn't planned—I found myself moving down the steps of the bleachers, closer to the ice. There was something magnetic about him, something I couldn't resist.

I needed to be nearer to get a better look. Watching from a distance wasn't enough—I wanted to be closer. The sharp hiss of his skates cutting into the ice echoed in the arena, and I swear, I felt it in my chest.

I stopped at the edge, my breath fogging the surface of the glass as I leaned closer, desperate to see more. He was entirely focused, his face set, and the intensity of his expression made my pulse quicken.

I needed to be closer. I needed to feel like I was in his orbit, even if he didn't know I was there and didn't understand why I couldn't stay away.

I wanted him to see me.

I was desperate for it.

But he didn't notice me at first. Blake gave me an exaggerated wave, then elbowed Noah as they broke for drinks.

Noah turned so fast I thought he'd fall on his ass, but no, he glided toward me, then stopped and indicated for me to walk to the gap near some benches.

He won't think I'm stalking him. Right?

"You're stalking me," he said, his voice sharp, the accusation cutting through the air between us like a slap.

I blinked, trying to keep my expression neutral. "I'm not *exactly* stalking you."

"Oh really?" Noah's brows shot up, his hands on his hips. He was still in his practice gear, his curls damp with sweat, and damn if he didn't look good while staring at me. "Because it sure seems like you've been everywhere I've been lately, Brody."

"I happened to be here," I said, shrugging as if my

pulse wasn't hammering. "It's a public place. People are allowed to watch hockey practice."

"Right," he said, crossing his arms. "You just happened to be at the rink in Harrisburg during practice. Just like you happened to show up at the karting. And you just happened to—"

"Okay, fine!" I threw up my hands, exhaling. "Maybe I was curious. But it's not stalking. I wasn't hiding in the shadows or planting a tracker on your car or whatever you think I'm doing."

His eyes widened in horror. "You're what now?"

"No, I'm not doing that."

Noah's expression softened a little, but his gaze still searched mine. "Why, Brody?"

The question hit harder than it should have. I hesitated, my gaze dropping to the polished floor. Why, indeed? Why couldn't I stay away from him? Why did I feel I could breathe easier around him, even if he glared at me as if I'd just keyed his car?

"I don't know," I admitted, my voice quieter. "I just… I wanted to see you."

Noah's stance relaxed, his arms uncrossing. "You could've just called."

My chest tightened, and I let out a dry laugh. "I don't have your number."

"You're a rich guy with endless contacts."

"Yeah, but it would have been weird. 'Hey, Noah, remember me? I got your number from my PI. I'm the guy you kissed, who then acted like an asshole? Want to hang out?'"

"You've hired a PI."

"No. I wouldn't. I'm not that guy."

"What do you want from me, Brody?"

"More kisses. Lunch. To talk. I don't know."

He tilted his head. "Okay, then, what do you need?" he asked.

For a moment, I couldn't answer. Because the truth—the pull I felt toward him, the way his presence calmed the chaos in my head—was too much to admit. Instead, I met his gaze, something raw and unspoken passing between us.

"I don't know," I said finally. "But it scares the hell out of me."

EIGHT

Noah

I FELT LIKE I WAS LIVING IN THAT OLD GENESIS SONG about the land of confusion that Pops was always singing.

Just when I'd started to wash that man right out of my hair—all the thanks to Mary Martin for her rendition of the song in *South Pacific*—here he was. And he looked a hundred different shades of bewildered with a splash of desperate longing. All of it aimed at me.

Did this guy seriously not get that I needed my head in the game right now? That I couldn't afford distractions—especially not from someone playing at being straight? Because no so-called "straight" guy I'd ever known—and I grew up surrounded by macho athletes, the real chest-thumping kind—had ever acted like that.

"Gunnarsson, are you planning to join us for this discussion of special teams or are you planning on relying on your genes to help you glide through this training camp?"

Coach Morin's deep voice slapped me in the back of the head like an errant puck. I jerked to attention, gave

Brody a dark-as-shit glower, and ground out a few words.

"We'll talk after practice."

With that, I skated back to the group of men kneeling at center ice, my cheeks hot with embarrassment.

"Sorry, Coach, personal stuff. It won't happen again," I apologized, knelt between Nik and Blake, and gave the talk about power plays my undivided attention.

We then worked on some quad passing drills, trying to hone our tape-to-tape passes as we were placed into makeshift lines. It was a simple drill, but an important one to work on, as a good power play was crucial to a good team, and the Railers' power play last year hadn't been great. I foresaw a lot of special teams' drills as the roster was whittled down day by day. Two guys had been sent down to the Colts already. To condition. A nice way of saying you're not ready. I did not want to hear that, if at all possible. I knew the odds weren't in my favor to make, let alone stay, on the roster this season. Brody Vance was a distraction that needed to step the hell off.

I worked twice as hard that practice. I had to. When Coach sent us to the showers, I was soaked in sweat, mad at myself, and more than a little irritated with *Speed Racer* rocking those aviator glasses and tight jeans. When we exited the locker room, there he was, deep in conversation with the GM of the team. The fucking general manager had raced—ha-ha—down here to our practice facility to talk with *the* Brody Vance. That had to be as rare as creating a perfect March Madness bracket.

Brody Vance was my white whale. He stalked my dreams and my waking moments, pushing me into doing stupid things that would see me being dragged to the dark, cold depths of career failure after I had harpooned him. Not only would I drown, but my ship and my crew would be smashed to smithereens leaving poor Ishmael (Ishmael aka Nikolai) clinging to the Zamboni for dear life until the ice crew could rescue him.

Dramatic much?

Uhm yeah, drama major.

"Noah, come over here a moment. I was just talking with Brody here about you," Paul Curtis called from his little chummy chum talk with Brody. Paul was a middle-aged man with a sports management degree under his belt and had been hired on to take us back to our glory days. Brown-hair, brown eyes, a little bit on the young side for a GM at just forty, he had a plan, as he liked to tell the press. I made my way over under the curious glances of my teammates. Paul and I shook hands as I smiled, a smile that nervous rookies wore when talking to the guy who could sell you off to another team while eating his bagel and cream cheese. "How's your father?"

"Which one?" I asked as Brody and I exchanged looks.

"Both," Paul chuckled as he pumped my hand. "The Railers have been an inclusive team ever since Tennant Rowe came out and made history," Paul gushed to Brody. Brody nodded along. My hand was finally dropped. "Noah, Brody here was telling me that his niece is also diabetic. And that gave me a wonderful idea for a community outreach program. What do you think about setting up a youth hockey program for kids with diabetes?"

"My charity, 17 Racing, would be happy to donate whatever may be needed," Brody chimed in.

What could I say? It was a solid idea. I already knew of a few non-profits offering summer camps for diabetic children.

"Sure, I'd be happy to do what I could for the program," I said instantly, making Paul beam.

"Wonderful. I'll leave you and Brody to discuss it. Nice to meet you, Brody. Feel free to visit anytime you're in the Harrisburg area."

"Will do; thanks, Paul."

Paul clapped my shoulder and latched onto Coach Morin for a talk Coach seemed less than thrilled to have.

"He seems nice," Brody said when he fell in by my side as we made our way to the players' exit. "I really didn't mean to pull you into any involvement in a charity. I just mentioned that my niece was diabetic, and how much I admired you for playing a rough sport like hockey while dealing with your illness. He kind of picked it up and ran with it."

"Yeah, GMs are like that," I replied, waiting for the security officer at the door to take a selfie with Brody. The midday sun broke out from behind a fat cloud to warm my face.

"You seem a bit awkward around me," Brody said, slipping on his sunglasses and a brand new Railers snapback cap. "I'd really like to talk to you, but if it's too uncomfortable, just let me know."

I blew out a breath, my eyes on that puffy cloud rolling by. I turned my attention to Brody, who was in hiding-his-face-from-the-world mode. Shoulders up, brim of his cap down, shades in place.

"Look, I'm not awkward about anything., It's you

who's all over the place. I'm just trying not to fulfill Fedallah's prophecy is all."

"Fedallah from *Moby Dick*?"

Shit, he read classics too. Okay, this guy was too much. "Yeah, never mind. I just…" I ran a hand through my damp curls. "Look, I think we just need to sort a few things out, yeah?"

"Yeah, I'd like that. Lunch somewhere?"

I should have insisted on somewhere public, so we didn't tumble into that maybe kissing thing he had mentioned. More kissing would be bad. I should stay away from the mouth of the whale, or I could get swallowed whole and have to spend three days in a whale gut with tons of plankton.

Great, now we're doing a mashup of Jonah and Moby D. You need to sort your head.

"My place," I offered instead of the public eatery, as a couple of folks from the cleaning staff began eyeballing Brody and whispering to each other. Yep, that was why I chose my place. Not because part of me was stuck on more kissing. Nope, it was *totally* the need for privacy. No other reason. I was being a good guy, and hockey players are known for being good guys. Pops and Dad would be proud of all my goodness. "Follow me."

He did—in a beater Toyota Corolla. It blended in way better than that fire engine red Maserati he'd been driving. My apartment complex was back in the city, about a thirty-minute ride from Carlisle, so I had plenty of time to think on the way home about what I would say to Brody. I was going to keep it simple—no fucking whale references—and tell him that while I liked him and his dick

—his dick was perfection—I wasn't in a place to be shuttled around while some "straight" dude figured himself out. I got it, I did—working out your sexuality was tough. I'd been there, done that; Pops bought me the t-shirt.

I had my speech all planned. I was pretty good at memorizing lines quickly. I could still recite my monologue from playing Paul in *A Chorus Line* in high school. This short little dialog I'd worked on as Brody followed behind me like a spinster aunt instead of his Lead Foot Larry usual mode of driving would be cake. Short cake. Ha. Oh, fuck I was stupid.

I pulled into my designated parking spot, and Brody slid into the guest space beside me. The Red Point Complex was a ten-story building overlooking the river, featuring some really nice units. My standard studio was a bit small, but it offered a great view of the Market Street Bridge. It was a clean place with high ceilings and a fantastic building manager named Cameron.

The lobby was typical apartment complex with a few couches, a wall of mailboxes, and a security officer at the desk. I had made a point to get to know the people who worked hard to keep the complex safe and clean, and called out a greeting to Mark, the tall man behind the desk. He waved hello and gave Brody a once-over.

"You need to register, sir," Mark said. I threw Brody a questioning glance. So, he removed his hat and glasses. Mark stared hard for a moment, then recognition dawned. "Oh shit…"

"I'd appreciate it if you kept my visit here just between the three of us?"

"Oh, yeah, sure. Were you *really* caught dating the wife of the team owner?"

"Don't believe everything you read," Brody tossed out with a smile, but I caught a glimpse of pain in his expression. I huffed, then went towards the elevators, leaving Brody to shake hands, then jogging to catch up, his hat back on his head. I sent him a sharp look. "What's wrong?"

"Nothing." I jammed my finger into the red button with the six on it, confused as hell about why I felt this flare of anger over Brody sleeping with some woman. I mean, if she was the wife of someone, that was shitty, obviously. But why should I care? He'd probably slept with a thousand women, all while giving guys the side-eye on the sly. Which was what I was. A sly side-eye.

"This may have been a bad idea," he muttered.

I turned from watching myself stew in the buffed walls of the elevator. Without thinking, I kissed him hard, right on the mouth. His body went rigid, and then, he began to soften into me. The *ping* of a bell and the lurch of the elevator stopping sliced into my haze enough to pull me back as the door opened. Brody stood there stunned, eyes wide, as two neighbors waited to step in.

"Hey," I said as I exited. Brody shielded his face with his hat as we strode down the brightly lit hall in tandem, neither of us saying a word. "This is me," I coughed out as I unlocked the door to 6-B and stepped inside. The place was tidy; the cleaning lady my father had hired when I moved in had just left. I could still smell the lemon Pledge she used to dust my coffee table. I chucked my keys onto a small table inside the door and turned to

Brody, who was checking out a few family portraits on the off-white wall.

His gaze darted from the shot of me, my fathers, and my sisters at my college graduation to me. I got lost in his eyes. They were the prettiest I had ever seen on a man. Long dark lashes framed the gray. He was a little shorter than me, so he had to look up a bit. My speech dissipated. I leaned down to taste his mouth again. There was no hesitation this time. No muscles stiffening in shock. Brody "I'm Straight as a Ruler" Vance was totally into this. So into it, he spun me around as if I wasn't five eleven, weighing in at one eighty four, and an athlete in my prime.

"More kissing," he growled as he carded his fingers into my hair so tight it almost made my eyes water. I met his tongue stroke for stroke, bending my knees and shoving my hands up under his shirt. The skin on his back was warm, soft, and covered tight muscle. God, I loved the feel of a man's power. Don't get me wrong, I loved the gentle roundness of a woman, too, but there was something about this man and his rawness that made me stupid.

We took a few turns manhandling each other against the wall, my hands now on his ass as he slanted my head just where he wanted it. He leaned in to rut his cock against my hip, and I saw stars. Then, the doorbell chimed a foot from where we were groping each other.

Brody jumped back, lips swollen, dick hard, eyes glazed with lust. I probably looked the same.

"Let me…" I jerked a thumb at the door.

He nodded, then walked into my living room. Spinning from him, I peered through the peep hole to see the paperboy on the other side. Right. Yeah. Cool. I tugged my shirt down to cover my boner, fished some bills from my front pocket, and shoved the cash at little Ronnie Lewis, who gaped at the huge tip.

"For exemplary paper delivery," I told him with a smile.

"Gee, thanks!" He raced down the hall. I shut the door, drew in a shaky breath, and turned to gaze upon the man pulling me deeper into the briny depths.

He was lost. I could relate. "I have food. We can eat. And talk. I think we should maybe not kiss again until after the talking."

"We do seem to have problems keeping our hands off each other." He glanced at me. I bobbed my head. "I've never really had this issue with a man before. I feel like I'm spinning out of control in a car I've never driven."

"I get it. I feel like I'm being tugged underwater by an ivory sperm whale." He cocked an eyebrow. It was a really attractive move on a beautiful man. I did not allow my inner voice to comment on the word sperm. Sometimes, my twelve-year-old boy managed to break free.

"Ah right, I'm your white whale," he commented. "I like your place. My house is very different. Clinical."

"I like my space."

"No one comes to mine... I mean... most people are put off by who I am, or want to meet Jemima, or hang on to my coattails because of my money or..." He winced as if he hadn't meant to say that at all. "Fuck, I have no social skills," he added and scrubbed his eyes.

"My sisters and aunt picked it out and did the decorating." I waved a hand at the nicely matched blue and tan sofa, armchairs, and throw rug on the floor. "When I signed my entry-level contract, I rented this place. Well, my fathers had to cosign, but yeah, it's mine. As for your money, please, I grew up around Tennant Rowe. Tate Collins is a family friend. I grew up in a mansion with a hockey rink on the grounds, a movie theater for watching Elvis flicks, and a garage filled with pink Cadillacs and Stutz Blackhawks."

"Good to know."

He stared some more at the photos, but I could tell he was preparing to say something. "It worries me how young you are," he said at last, as if he were as old as my parents.

"I'm *literally* seven years younger than you," I huffed as I made my way to the kitchen.

"I've lived a lot of life," he murmured, following me into the tiny food prep area. It was a sunny space, with herbs on the windowsill that Dad had to remind me to water every week.

"Not as much life as me it seems?"

"Maybe not."

"How about we discuss some of that life," I replied, then opened the fridge. "You good with a green goddess salad with chicken?" I asked over my shoulder.

"Sounds good." He was an athlete. Or was. That whole retirement thing seemed odd, too; he got squirrely whenever someone mentioned it.

"Cool," Brody said behind me as I started pulling ingredients from the fridge: kale, peppers, tomatoes, cucumber, and avocado. I grabbed some bell peppers and set them on the counter before digging through the drawer for a knife.

I could feel him watching as I moved around the kitchen, but I tried to ignore it. Cooking wasn't exactly thrilling, but I liked it—simple and predictable. I washed the veggies and started chopping, falling into an easy rhythm as the sound of the knife hitting the cutting board filled the space.

"You have to eat more carefully, I guess. Because of diabetes?" Brody asked, leaning against the counter, his arms crossed as he watched me dice a tomato. "No huge plates of pasta?"

I shrugged. "Pretty much. It's not that different from what any professional athlete eats. High protein, good carbs, healthy fats. Balance is key, especially when I'm training or playing." He nodded, his gray eyes tracking every movement as if I were a puzzle he was trying to figure out. I grabbed a bowl and tossed the chopped veggies in. "It's about timing. Eating before games or practices ensures I've got enough energy, but not so much that my blood sugar spikes. And then, after, I have to refuel to recover."

I pulled out some leftover roasted chicken, shredded it with my hands, and added it to the bowl. "It's a lot of trial and error, but I've been doing it long enough to know what works for me."

Brody tilted his head, curiosity flickering in his expression. "My niece has an insulin pump. She's had diabetes since she was two."

"Aww, bless her." I grabbed a handful of almonds and tossed them into the bowl, my focus on the salad. Brody sat across the counter, watching me with that quiet, curious intensity that made me feel as if I were under a microscope.

"Do you use a pump?" he asked, his gaze flicking down to where my shirt had risen, exposing a sliver of skin.

I shook my head. "Nope. Hockey's too rough for one. Pumps are great, but they're delicate. One bad hit, a fall, or even just getting slammed into the boards the wrong way and it could get ripped out. It's not worth the risk; I use multiple daily injections. Long-acting insulin once a day, fast-acting before meals and as needed. It works for me."

Brody leaned forward, resting his elbows on the counter. "So, no automatic adjustments? No steady stream?"

"Nope. It's all manual. I have to check my blood sugar, count my carbs, and decide how much insulin to take." I smirked. "It's like having a full-time job on top of my actual full-time job."

Brody was silent for a moment, his fingers drumming against the counter. "Avery hates her pump," he admitted. "She says it's itchy and doesn't feel normal."

I nodded, scraping the avocado into the salad. "Yeah, I get that. It's a lot, especially for a kid. Some people love their pumps, but they're not for everyone. I had one for a while when I was younger, but I hated feeling like I had something attached to me all the time."

Brody studied me, his gray eyes sharp but unreadable. "Doesn't it get exhausting? Managing all of it?"

I shrugged. "It's just my normal. I don't think about it much—it's like breathing. You just do it."

He exhaled, shaking his head. "I don't know how you do it."

I smiled, handing him a fork and setting the salad bowl between us. "Same way you survived years of F1. Discipline, routine, and pure stubbornness."

Brody huffed a laugh, shaking his head. "Yeah, I guess we've both had to figure out how to stay alive."

The words sat between us, heavy but unspoken. He wasn't just talking about diabetes, and I wasn't just talking about racing.

We just understood each other.

He nodded slowly, and for a moment, his expression softened. "You're a good role model, you know? For kids like my niece."

The compliment caught me off guard, and I ducked my head, focusing on the dressing I was whisking together—parsley, garlic, lemon juice, and buttermilk. "Thanks," I said, my voice quieter than I intended.

I poured the dressing over the salad, tossing it until everything was coated. Then, I grabbed two plates and served it. When I turned back to him, he was still watching me, his expression unreadable but intense.

"All right," I said, handing him a plate. "Dinner's ready. No complaints about the kale, okay?"

He took the plate with a small smile, his fingers brushing mine briefly. "No promises," he said, but his tone was lighter now as we sat at the tiny island, a tiny one for two. After filling two water glasses, we dove into our salads.

"This is *really* good," he said after a few bites.

"Thanks. I took a few cooking classes in college, just

trying to learn how to feed myself now that I didn't have two parents watching every bite I ate. I like cooking and feeding people. It's nice to see someone enjoy what you make."

"You're not at all like I would've imagined a hockey player to be," he said, then dabbed at his chin with a paper napkin. The afternoon sun warmed the room.

"What did you think hockey players were like?" I asked, then took a bite of chicken. I suspected I already knew what he was going to say.

"Big dumb brutes who like to fight."

"That's candid. And totally wrong. I mean, sure, back in the old days you had goons trawling the ice just looking for a face to punch, but the game now is about speed and skill. Although, a hearty shoulder check is always a good thing."

"So, I'm learning."

I poked at a slice of cuke smothered in dressing. "I'm not sure where I sit with you."

"Beside me at the moment," he said, then gave my knee a gentle knock with his.

"Yeah, obviously, but I meant with where you are inside your head." I looked right at him, my cuke still hanging off my fork. "I like kissing you, I do, and I could get into doing more, but I'm not going to screw up what I've worked for all my life over some guy who wants to touch my dick one second, then tells me in his next breath that he's not into guys. I don't have time for that, you know. I'm working my ass off to make the team. So, if you're going to stay in your little cloud of denial, cool, have fun with that, but leave me out of it. My future is too important to me to expend all that mental output on a guy who won't give me what I need emotionally." He blinked at me as if he'd taken a puck to the noggin. "Sorry if that was too blunt, but I've danced this troika before. Dudes that can't cop to being attracted to the same sex to the world but want to get their dicks sucked by a guy. So, if you're going to keep being cagey, this lunch is probably the last time you'll eat with me or kiss me. You hearing me?"

"You're quite mature," he said softly. "In many ways, you're way more together than I am."

"I've just had more time to come to know myself. I was crushing on guys when I was thirteen. And I grew up with two dads and a trans sister. Our house was Rainbow Central all year round, so when I started pinning up Jensen Ackles pics next to my Sabrina Carpenter posters, they were both like yep, we got a bi-boy."

I smiled at the memory of how cool my fathers had been. I'd been incredibly fortunate to grow up surrounded by inclusivity.

"That's amazing. My story is vastly different."

"Well yeah, you dated a popstar." He winced at that, and part of me wished I could take the words back, so I changed the subject. "Why don't you tell me your story? We have lots of salad." I gave his knee a bump and got a smile that made me wonder if living under the sea might not be that bad.

NINE

Brody

I DIDN'T WANT TO DO THIS, SO TO AVOID ANSWERING immediately, I took the bowls to the sink as if the world depended on my washing up.

"Brody?" Noah prompted and tugged me around, so I faced him.

"Didn't you Google me?" I asked, leaning back against the counter, arms crossed.

Noah shook his head, one of his curls bouncing free from behind his ear. "I'm not a stalker like you," he teased.

I huffed a laugh, staring at the floor for a second before shrugging.

Where did I start? Right at the beginning? Or with the news I'd been living with since last November? Doc had finished the appointment—no change blah blah, but then, he'd paused and added the kicker.

"I need you to understand the long-term implications. Even if the aneurysm remains stable, it will not go away. You may eventually need surgery. And if that happens,

there's a chance it could affect your motor skills. Your coordination. Possibly even your speech."

Yeah, telling Logan that wasn't happening, and I wasn't laying that on Noah. He was my focus, my sunshine, my hope, and I refused to add that shit to the already steaming pile of crap I was about to lay on him.

I wanted him to like me as a strong man, not someone with a ticking time bomb in their head.

I want him to kiss me.

Take me to bed.

Make me forget.

I cleared my throat. "Okay, so long story short, my grandfather was a Formula One racer in the eighties—Jason Vance." I waited for Noah to recognize the name, but he shook his head. "Well, he won a world championship and built a small empire on his celebrity. He put his work first. Had my dad—his only son—who married my mom, a Brazilian model. Picture-perfect life, right?"

I glanced at him. Noah wasn't smirking anymore. His brows had drawn together, and his face shifted through several emotions. I ignored the fact that he was picking up on the unspoken stuff, or reading things into what I was saying, and pressed on.

"My dad was a racer, like me. He never had a chance to make it big, though. Lots of pressure on him from his dad. He drank, smoked, took drugs, slept around, and enjoyed all the trappings of too much money and not enough sense."

"Ouch."

"Yeah, well, my mom filed for divorce when I was

five. They reconciled a couple of years later, but it was messy. If you want the details, it's in every media post about me." I waved a hand as if I was dismissing all that shit.

Noah stayed silent, but the way his eyes narrowed, and lips pressed together told me he was biting back a comment. I kept going.

"So, I have an older brother, Logan, and he's my best friend. He's married to Sadie and is Avery's dad. He turned his back on a career in driving, got thrown out of the house by my grandfather, and cut off from the family money, but survived. He's now my agent, so that's a fuck-you to the old man."

"Brody—"

I forged ahead. "But there's also my other brother…" I swallowed—the pain of childhood loss was still there. "Charlie was two years younger than me."

"'Was'?"

This was always the hardest part, and I swallowed, the words sticking slightly. "Mom, Dad, and Charlie died in a light aircraft accident when I was seven. Dad was piloting —he'd been drinking or was high. End of story."

Noah's face was a storm of emotions now—pity, sadness, anger, and something else I couldn't name. He stared at me like he was trying to determine if I was messing with him.

I didn't want his pity. I didn't want to make him sad or angry. I didn't want any of that.

"Jesus, Brody," he said after a long pause, his voice quiet but heavy. "That's… a lot."

I shrugged again, keeping my expression neutral. "It is what it is."

"No, it's not," he snapped, his brows furrowing deeper. "It's not just 'what it is.' You were seven, and your dad—" He bit his lip as if he wasn't sure how far to go.

"It's fine," I said. "It was a long time ago."

"It's not fine," Noah said, his voice softer now, but still full of frustration. "And you saying it like that doesn't make it fine."

I glanced at him, his expression open, raw, and unguarded. "What do you want me to say?" I asked, my tone sharper than I intended. "That it screwed me up? That I still think about it every day. Because I don't. My biggest rival wasn't on the track, but in my own family, and proving myself made me strong and a winner." My chest was tight because I wasn't a fucking winner. I had no clue what I was doing with whatever remained of my disordered life.

Noah's lips parted as if he wanted to argue, but he kept quiet, studying me. Finally, he said, "I'm sorry."

I let out a dry laugh. "Don't be. It's not your fault."

"No," he said, his voice steady now. "But it still sucks. And I'm still sorry."

I didn't know what to say, so I said nothing. Noah's gaze stayed on me. For once, I didn't feel the need to look away.

"Tell me what your grandfather did to you," Noah said, calm but unrelenting.

"That's between me and my therapist," I shot back. "Sorry, I didn't mean…"

Noah didn't flinch. "Does he know you're attracted to men?"

"I'm not. It's just you... it's..." I scrubbed my eyes. "No, he doesn't."

Noah tilted his head, studying me with that steady gaze of his. "Why not?"

I let out a bitter laugh, running a hand through my hair. "Because he has plans for me, okay? World champion, legacy, a stunning woman by my side, creating a brand-new generation of Vance kids to carry on the name. That's the plan. His plan." I could feel the weight of it pressing down on me, every expectation he'd drilled into me since I was a kid. "He made me the best driver I could be," I continued, my voice growing quieter. "He forged me out of bitterness as if I was a weapon he could wield."

Noah stayed quiet, but I could see his jaw tightening, his hands curling into fists at his sides.

"And now?" I whispered, my voice breaking. "Now I'm just..."

My legs gave way, and before I knew it, I was sliding down the wall, the cold surface biting into my back until I hit the floor. I rested my arms on my knees, staring at the space between my feet as the words tumbled out, raw and unfiltered.

"Used up and fucking lost."

The silence that followed was heavy, but Noah didn't leave. He didn't try to fix it or fill the space with meaningless platitudes. Instead, he crouched in front of me, his expression fierce, grounding me in a way I didn't know I needed.

"You're not done, Brody." His steady voice was full of

conviction. "You just need to figure out what you want—not what he wants or anyone else expects. You."

I swallowed hard, my chest tightening even more. I wanted to believe him, but the truth was, I didn't know where to start. Maybe I should start with the one thing I could decide.

"I want you for however long I can have you."

Noah's eyes widened, a flicker of surprise crossing his face before it softened into something warmer. He scooted forward, crossing his legs in front of me, our knees almost touching.

"Okay," he murmured, reaching to cup my face with his hand. His thumb brushed across my cheekbone, sending a shiver down my spine.

I leaned into his touch, feeling the warmth of his palm against my skin, and before I could second-guess myself, I closed the distance between us. The kiss was tentative—I was afraid this moment might shatter if we moved too fast. But then, Noah's hand slid to the back of my neck, pulling me closer, and the kiss deepened. His lips were warm and insistent against mine, and I felt something inside me begin to unravel.

I reached out, my fingers tangling in the fabric of his shirt, desperate to anchor myself to him as he kissed me back. The cold of the cupboard door at my back faded away, replaced by the heat of Noah's body as he pressed closer.

When we finally broke apart, breathing heavily, I rested my forehead against his. Noah's eyes were dark, pupils dilated, and a flush had spread across his cheeks.

He looked as dazed as I felt, and something about that steadied me.

"I shouldn't be doing this," I admitted. "I'm selfish and stupid."

"If you're going to tell me the kiss was a mistake…" Noah shuffled back, but I caught his wrist before he could move. My heart raced.

"No," I said, my voice hoarse. "That's not what I meant."

Noah paused, his eyes searching mine, and I tugged on his arm, pulling him towards me.

"I meant I shouldn't be doing this because I'm a mess," I explained, my words coming out in a rush. "But I want to. God, Noah, I want to so much."

"Sex is just that. It doesn't have to mean anything, Brody."

"I know."

Relief flooded his features, and he moved, closing the distance between us. I guided him onto my lap, my hands settling on his hips as he straddled me, his weight warm and solid.

This time, when our lips met, there was no hesitation. I slid my hands under Noah's shirt, exploring warm skin as he pressed closer. His fingers tangled in my hair, and I groaned into his mouth.

We broke apart for air, both panting. Noah's forehead rested against mine, his breath hot on my face. I could feel the rapid beat of his heart where our chests pressed together.

"Brody," he whispered.

I surged forward, capturing his mouth again. My tongue traced the seam of his lips, and he opened for me. As we kissed, Noah rocked his hips, creating delicious friction. I gasped, breaking the kiss to trail my lips down his face.

Noah's head fell back, exposing more of his neck as I kissed and nipped the sensitive skin. His hands gripped my shoulders, fingers digging in as he ground down against me. I bucked my hips up to meet his movements, groaning at the feel of him hard against my belly.

"God, Brody," Noah panted, voice rough with need. "You feel so good."

I captured his lips again, swallowing his moans as we rocked together. My hands slid down to grip his ass, guiding his movements as we rutted. The heat between us built, tension, coiling tighter with each thrust.

My hand slipped beneath the waistband of Noah's sweatpants, fingers grazing skin. He gasped into my mouth, hips jerking at the contact. I wrapped my hand around his cock.

"Is this okay?" I murmured, searching his face.

"Please, don't stop," he pleaded.

I stroked him, reveling in the way he shuddered. His head fell to my shoulder, breath hot on my neck as he panted. I could feel him trembling, little whimpers escaping with each movement of my hand.

"Brody," he moaned, voice muffled. His hips rocked, pushing into my grip. "I'm close, I'm gonna—"

I tightened my hold.

Noah's words cut off with a gasp as I quickened my pace, twisting my wrist on the upstroke. His body went taut, muscles trembling as he approached the edge. I pressed open-mouthed kisses along his neck, tasting the salt of his skin.

"Let go," I murmured into his ear. "I've got you."

With a choked cry, Noah came undone. He shuddered in my arms, spilling hot and wet over my hand. I stroked him through it, gentling my touch as he whimpered at the oversensitivity.

As Noah's breathing evened out, he lifted his head from my shoulder. His face was flushed, eyes hazy with pleasure. He cupped my face in his hands, kissing me deeply.

"You didn't come," he whispered against my lips, lifting his ass a little, then pressing down again.

"It's okay."

"It's not okay. I'm a gentleman." He smiled at me, cheeky, flushed, and so damn sexy.

I couldn't help but chuckle at Noah's words. "A gentleman, huh?" I teased; voice rough with want.

Noah's smile widened, a mischievous glint in his eyes. "Oh yes," he purred, rocking his hips. "My dads brought me up the right way, and a gentleman always ensures his partner's satisfaction."

Before I could respond, Noah was sliding off my lap. He knelt between my legs, hands running up my thighs as he looked up at me through his lashes. My breath caught.

"Let me take care of you," Noah murmured, toying with the waistband of my pants. "Please?"

I nodded, unable to form words, as Noah pulled down my zipper. His hand slipped inside, wrapping around my length, and I groaned at the contact.

"God, Noah," I muttered, hips bucking involuntarily.

He smiled, leaning forward to press a kiss to the tip of my cock. My head fell back to the wall with a thud as Noah's warm mouth enveloped me. His tongue swirled around the head before he took me deeper, hollowing his cheeks as he sucked.

I threaded my fingers through Noah's curls, not guiding, just needing something to hold on to as pleasure overwhelmed me. He hummed, the vibrations sending shockwaves through my body.

Noah's free hand cupped my balls, rolling them as he bobbed his head. The dual sensation was almost too much, and I could feel my orgasm building way too fast.

"Noah," I gasped, tugging at his hair in warning. "I'm close."

Instead of pulling away, Noah redoubled his efforts. He took me deeper, the tip of my cock hitting the back of his throat. His eyes flicked up to meet mine, dark with desire, and that was my undoing.

I came hard with a strangled cry, shuddering as waves of pleasure crashed over me. Noah swallowed around me, working me through my orgasm until I whimpered.

He released me with a *pop*, pressing a gentle kiss to my hip before crawling back into my lap. I wrapped my arms around him, holding him close as we both caught our breath.

"Was that gentlemanly enough for you?" Noah asked, a teasing lilt to his voice.

"More than enough," I said, pulling Noah closer and pressing a kiss to his temple. "You're amazing. You know that?"

Noah hummed, nuzzling my neck. "So are you," he murmured against my skin.

We sat there for a while, tangled together on the floor, our breathing returning to normal. The weight of Noah in my arms felt right in a way I couldn't explain.

"What happens now?" I asked, voicing the question lurking at the edges of my mind.

Noah lifted his head to look at me, his eyes warm and sincere. "Whatever we want to happen," he said.

"I'm not out; I'm…"

"Closeted, I get that. It's the nature of the job, sponsorship, management, and all that crap. Up until my Uncle Ten, well, hockey was a bad place to be queer, then my dads came out, and the Railers became this safe place."

"Can you be my safe place for a while? Is that too much to ask? I'm so fucking sorry I can't give you more, but this… I'm sorry, Noah."

Noah's expression softened, and his eyes shone with emotion. He gently cupped my face, his thumbs stroking my cheekbones. "Don't be sorry. We can be friends," he murmured. "I'm here."

"Just friends?" I asked with a smile.

"Friends with benefits," he said in complete seriousness, then pressed his nose to mine and bopped it.

I leaned into his touch, feeling a lump form in my throat at the sincerity in his voice. "I don't know how to do this," I admitted. "I've never… with a guy…"

"You seem to manage okay," Noah teased.

I twisted my finger through one of his curls. He was sunshine and happiness, and I was…

… fuck knows what I was.

"This can't last," I said.

"It's okay," Noah assured me, kissing my forehead. "One day, you might tell the world, and we'll be a thing that matters. Or you won't; I'll want more, and it ends. Either way, it will be okay for a while."

I nodded. I wished that world was now. I wished I was brave enough to destroy people's perceptions of me. I wished everyone would leave me alone. I wished I had time. I wrapped my arms around him, and he nestled in my arms. Even though this floor was hard and cold, I never wanted to leave this space.

"We should move and clean up," Noah murmured, jumping up before extending a hand to help me. We took turns in the bathroom before moving to the sofa, and then, the roles were reversed; it was me cuddling into him.

TEN

Noah

BLAKE AND NIK WERE DISCUSSING THE LATEST NEWS ON football as we lifted.

The gym was alive with players building muscle and endurance, working their asses off to grab every microsecond of advantage they could get. Most of the vets were secure. Many had no-move or no-trade clauses, so while they also were putting in the work, it wasn't as frenzied as the rookies or the couple of guys here on waivers who were also trying to make the cut.

"Add another ten," I panted as I lay flat on my back staring at the ceiling and soaked in sweat.

"You sure? You're already at fifty over half your weight," Blake replied, football talk ending as both of my linemates stared down at me. The monitor hooked to my wrist was recording every lift, then sending it to a software program the coaching staff used to monitor our workouts. "If you push too hard they're going to come down on you for exerting yourself past what the docs have recommended for you."

"Strength on bench equals success on ice," I stated and got eyerolls.

"Dude, seriously? Benching is not the be all and end all. Just do your one-fifty for twenty reps. Or do you want to blow out your labrum and rotators?"

"Legs feed the wolf," Nik interjected.

It kind of pissed me off that they were hassling me but whatever. I sat up, grabbed my towel, and scrubbed my face. My arms were burning anyway. And yeah, they were right. If I overdid training, the coaches and docs would freak out.

"You are beast monster. No worries." Nik nudged me off the bench, wiped it down with a disinfecting wipe, then splayed his big body over it, planting his feet soundly. "Spot me, if any of you pamby-mamby can lift bar."

"What a shit-stirrer," I joked, then took a second to check my numbers. Fuck. Yeah, I had pushed it harder than I should, and my numbers were showing it. I knew better. Overtraining made the muscle less sensitive to insulin, which made it difficult to utilize glucose properly. My levels were higher than I'd like. I tugged my shirt down with a sigh.

"I'm going to get some water and take some insulin. My sugar is kind of high," I told the guys. Both got that terrified look. "It's fine. I'm not going to DKA or anything. Just need to get the numbers down. Spot him. Go on, it's cool. Happens all the time."

To be honest, it didn't happen all the time. But it did happen on occasion.

"Okay, we'll check on you after morning skate. See if

you want to go visit that new Mexican place a few blocks over."

"Cool." I smiled my brightest smile, then left the gym, tossing my sweaty towel into the bin as I nodded at Cap on the way out.

Hiding the fatigue that was setting in, I dipped into the locker room, got my kit, and measured out a dosage. I chose my upper arm for the injection. Then, it was a waiting game. I emptied a bottle of water and opened a music app as I chilled. The rapid-acting insulin usually worked fast, so within ten or fifteen minutes, I should be good to go. After cleaning the syringe and shit, I had time to think. Probably not a good thing. Brody always popped up when I had spare time to meditate. Also, the latest release from Jemima was playing on my phone. It was still pretty wild to think that my new guy had dated one of the most popular singers in the world. They'd made a beautiful couple.

I wondered what his fans would think when they found out we were dating. I mean I was no Jemima Wren. She had me beat in just about every category of coolness and hotness imaginable. I could maybe skate better than she could, but other than that Jemima wiped the floor with me. I leaned back to rest on my locker, my head full of odd bits of worry that never seemed to go away. Was the world ready for someone like Brody to be with a guy? Progress had been made, but for every step forward, it seemed true equality took two steps back. How would the Railers react if I openly dated a man? Sure, it was one thing to be all supportive of a bisexual guy when he was wheeling chicks, but would the team be cool if I showed up at a fundraiser with Brody Vance on my arm?

Anxiety crept in, and so I left the locker room to find Coach. He was in his office, scouring over some video, the door open as it always was. Coach Morin wanted the players to know they could come to him at any time. I rapped on the doorframe. His dark brown eyes lifted from his laptop.

"Noah, did you need me?" he asked, and I nodded. Worry crinkled his brow. "Are you having some sort of medical issues?"

"No, I'm good. I was a little fatigued after a big workout, but I have things under control."

"Good, good. So, what can I do for you?"

I crept into the sunny office, closed the door, and took a seat in front of his desk. Coach wasn't the tidiest of men. His desk was littered with gum wrappers, empty coffee mugs, and playbooks. There were pictures of his wife and adult daughters. Two frames filled with shots of him and his grandkids.

"Your grandkids are cute," I said to try to ease into my reason for sitting here taking up his time with bullshit. Maybe I should have sat in the locker room a bit longer.

"Thanks, they're the apple of my eye. So, you're here to talk about my grandkids?" he prompted. I shook my head. "Do we need a player rep in here?"

"No, I don't... no. I was just... okay so I was just wondering how the team would feel if I started dating a guy. Publicly."

The tension around his mouth lessened. "Well, speaking only for myself, but I'm sure the rest of the organization would feel the same, we'd be fine with the son of two happily married men who played for our team for many years dating a man."

Oh yeah, right. Fathers. Plural. "Okay, yeah, sure. I guess that makes sense."

"Listen, I know that people are still people. Meaning that some fans are going to be twits no matter what year it is." I smiled at his frankness. Coach was nothing if not straightforward. I liked that about him. "The Railers have been an inclusive and safe team for many, many years. I do not see that changing anytime soon. So, if you want to bring a man to the next public activity, do so. Just make sure he trims his nose hair and wears a clean tie."

I chuckled. "Will do. Thanks, Coach." I rose, and we shook hands.

"No problem. Now get out of here and go shower. You smell like the inside of a gym bag left in the sun for a few days."

Shit. "Sorry. I'm out. Thanks again." I hauled my rank body back to the locker room, showered, and was pulling on my jeans when my phone buzzed. The din of men talking and laughing was a familiar one. Morning skate had been good, the team was coming together, and I was still here. My bout of silliness aside, the day was shaping up to be a good one.

I gave the text that had come in a fast read.

Pops and I have to go to Maryland overnight for a signing event. Can you come over and feed, then, let the dogs out?– Dad

As the Baja Men would say - I'll let the dogs out. 😊 *~ N*

Dad replied with a string of laughing emojis and a warm thank you.

"Hey, you feeling better?" Blake asked as he sat down on my left in a towel and purple Crocs with tiny ducks on them. Nik, a blatant exhibitionist, took a stance beside me, arms folded, dick swinging free for all the world to see.

"I would be if his junk wasn't in my face," I said, then jerked a thumb at the cocky Russian snickering.

"He is jealous of my big penis," Nik said as he wandered off to make small talk with Cap.

Blake nudged me in the side. "Your numbers cool?"

"Yeah, thanks. You were right. I shouldn't let the stress get to me."

"Correct. Which is why you should come to the movies with us tonight. Nik is lining up some girls for us, or you know, you can bring a dude. We're going to go see that new horror flick about the mutant Pekinese that attacks a small town."

Nope, that was a hard pass for me. I hated horror movies. Although a movie date with Brody would be nice. Only problem was that we were still hiding *us*.

"Did you say Pekinese? Like a tiny dog?" I asked when the full impact of what he had said sank in.

"Yeah, it sounds stupid, but Nik thinks the girls will be scared and need big strong hockey players to protect them." Blake shrugged. "So, if you have a guy you want to bring, feel free."

"I think I'll pass. Thanks though."

"Any time." He gave my shoulder a bump with the side of his fist, then moseyed back to his locker. The thought of a night out at the theater ate at me, so, being the clever man I am, I used the tried and true method that every teen uses. Folks are gone, and I have a key to the mansion. Not that I was a teen anymore, but if something works and all that.

I texted Brody and told him we were heading to the cinema tonight.

His reply was a line of about forty question marks.

Good. Let him wonder. It would be more fun when I showed him Pops' basement.

"This is... well, this is something else," Brody said as we entered the basement-slash-movie theater. Five dogs pranced around us, all fed and watered and back from a long run on the extensive grounds. "The interior has a very Vegas feel."

"Yeah, it does." I reached down to pick up Mittens from the raucous gaggle of dogs vying for even more attention. "In case you couldn't tell, my pops likes Elvis."

"I noticed," he answered with a cute smile.

It was hard not to notice. The red and black walls and ceiling were made to match the tones of Elvis's bedroom in Graceland. Over the scarlet walls were framed movie posters from several dozen of who knows how many movies Elvis made. Well, Pops would know. I had no clue. There was a popcorn machine, a soda fountain, and a pinball machine in the far corner that had an image of the King from his '68 comeback special. Yes, I knew that special well.

"You want some popcorn before the movie begins?" I

asked as we stepped over and around dogs, Mittens lying over my shoulder like a purring sandbag.

"Is it a good snack for you?" He flopped down into a plush padded seat in the first row. There were four, with ten seats in each row. Just in case a party of Elvis fans arrived at the front door. You never knew.

"It is." I handed him the cat, then fired up the machine as he leaned back, legs out, hands clasped behind his head. He looked so peaceful. It was a really nice look on him. When the corn was finished popping, I scooped up two paper bags full, delivered them, then went to the soda fountain. Brody and I both decided on cold water, extra ice. Once we were all settled–the dogs each taking one recliner, Brody, me, and then Mittens on the back of my seat–I cued up the digital film and sound system on my phone. "So, I talked to Coach today. About my, potentially, at maybe some future time, having a public boyfriend. And he was like dude, your fathers are married and half of our alumni are queer. It'll be fine."

"Oh, wow, that's amazing." He glanced over after taking a sip of cold water. "I'm just… I guess I'm stunned. I've not heard any positive feedback of any kind when it came to being out for a racer. I've only seen closed doors."

"No closed doors on the Railers. I'll make the team based on my skills on ice, with no red marks for being bisexual." I felt pretty darn good about that, but Brody still seemed a little unsure, so as not to push too hard and too fast, I switched topics. "Okay, so the only drawback to this theater is that Pops only has Elvis movies downloaded to his account. But I know one that you'll really think is super groovy daddy-o."

"Bring it on," he said as the lights dimmed and *Speedway* began to play.

"Nancy Sinatra is in this one," I said. "She's slinky."

I'd seen this movie at least twenty times. And hey, a foxy girl is a foxy girl, no matter what decade it was.

He leaned over to steal a kiss. "Still thinking of Nancy?"

I took a moment to ponder. "Yeah, I think so. You better kiss me again."

He did. Three times to be exact. And that seemed to purge Ms. Sinatra from my head for the rest of the movie. Of course, when she sang "Your Groovy Self," he had to kiss me a lot more.

Yeah, movie date nights were pretty awesome.

ELEVEN

Brody

THE RINK WAS EERILY QUIET AT FIVE IN THE MORNING, with the kind of silence that felt both calming and surreal. Noah unlocked the side door and flicked on the lights, illuminating the pristine sheet of ice stretching before us. It was a perfect, untouched, blank canvas.

"Trust me," Noah said, his smile soft but sure as he handed me a pair of skates.

I held them as if they might bite. "I've never done this," I warned, though the prospect of trying something new with him was more enticing than I cared to admit.

"You'll be fine," he said, crouching to lace up his skates. His movements were practiced and efficient, every flick of his wrist reminding me how much of his life had been spent on the ice.

I followed his lead, fumbling as I tightened the laces. By the time I stood up, my ankles already felt wobbly.

Noah glanced over and grinned. "Come on," he said, holding out a hand.

I took it, letting him guide me to the rink's edge. My

legs felt foreign, every step awkward and unsure, but his grip was steady, grounding me.

"All right, ready?" Noah asked, stepping effortlessly onto the ice.

"Not even a little," I muttered, but I followed him anyway, placing one skate onto the slick surface, then the other.

"Relax," he encouraged, skating backward a few feet so he could face me. "You're overthinking it. Just... let go."

I wanted to argue, but something about how he stared at me—patient, confident, sure—made me trust him. Taking a deep breath, I pushed off, wobbled, and nearly fell, but Noah was there, his hands steadying me.

"See? You're fine," he said, grinning as I found my balance.

"Fine is a stretch," I replied, but I was moving... slowly but surely.

It didn't take long before the initial awkwardness began to fade. Noah skated beside me, his movements fluid and natural, and I mimicked his rhythm, gaining confidence with each lap. The ice felt different from anything I'd ever experienced—not as fast as a car, but smooth in a way that made me feel both out of control and alive.

"It's... fast," I said, my voice echoing in the empty rink. "But smooth. On some tracks, the car vibrates so hard I can barely get out after a session. This is... different."

Noah glanced over, his smile softening. "Do you miss it?"

I didn't answer right away. Instead, I let the question

hang between us as we glided around the rink, the quiet hiss of our skates the only sound. Eventually, we stopped and leaned against the barrier, catching our breath.

"Yes," I sighed. "And no. I miss driving fast. I miss the adrenaline rush, the way everything else disappears when you're behind the wheel. But I don't miss the pressure, the insanity, the secrets."

Noah's expression was thoughtful as he nodded, his gaze fixed on the ice in front of us. "I get that," he said. "Sometimes, I think about what it'll be like when I'm done with hockey. If I'll miss it or... if I'll be glad to leave it behind."

"You've got time," I said, nudging his shoulder. "You're just getting started."

He smiled, but something in his eyes told me he was already thinking about the future.

"Come on," he said after a moment, straightening. "Let's go a few more laps. You're starting to look like you know what you're doing."

"Careful," I teased, pushing off from the barrier. "You'll give me a big head."

"Too late," he shot back, laughing as he skated ahead, daring me to catch him.

I tried, but Noah was a professional, his movements effortless as he circled the rink. Whenever I thought I was gaining on him as he skated lazily, he'd pick up speed, a mischievous grin lighting his face. He was probably skating at two percent of what he could really do.

"Come on, Brody!" he called over his shoulder. "Is that all you've got?"

"Don't push your luck," I muttered, but I couldn't help

the smile tugging at my lips. No matter how hard I pushed, I couldn't catch him. He finally slowed, skating back toward me.

"All right," he said, his breath fogging in the cold air. "Let's try something different."

Before I could ask what he meant, he grabbed my hands and pulled me closer. "What are you doing?" I asked though I didn't resist.

"Dancing," he said, spinning me in a slow circle.

"I'm not sure this counts as dancing," I said, laughing despite myself.

"Trust me," he murmured, his hands steady as he guided me. The motion was smooth, gliding as he twirled me. It felt like we were in our own little world for a moment, the rest of the rink fading away, and somehow, he even managed to sneak in a kiss.

But then, the dizziness hit. It started as a faint buzz behind my eyes, growing sharper with each spin until I had to pull away, gripping his arms.

"Noah, stop," I said, my voice more strained than intended.

He stopped, his expression shifting to concern. "What is it? Are you okay?"

I pressed my fingers to my temples, the dull ache spreading through my skull. "Just… give me a second. Got a headache starting, that's all."

"Shit, Brody," he said, his hands steadying me. "Why didn't you say something?"

"Because I didn't know until two seconds ago," I replied, trying to smile through the discomfort.

He guided me off the ice, his arm around my shoulders

as we returned to the bench. "Sit," he said, pulling a water bottle from his bag and handing it to me.

"It's not a big deal," I said, though the throbbing in my temples begged to differ.

Noah crouched in front of me, his gaze steady and serious. "I shouldn't have spun you so fast."

"I liked that," I murmured.

Noah shook his head, already unlacing my skates with care. I stared at the top of his head, at the messy blond curls, catching the glint of the rink's lights in his hair. I reached out, threading my fingers through the strands, letting the motion ground me. My headache was still there, a persistent thrum at my temples, but touching him, focusing on him, pushed the fear back.

Was this it? Was this the bomb inside my head, ready to explode? Was Noah the last thing I was going to see? My chest tightened, my mouth went dry, and the throbbing in my skull felt unbearable for a moment. Why hadn't I told him? What would he do if I collapsed right here? It would kill him to see someone die in front of him. I should have told him…

The panic clawed at my throat, but then, I felt the silky texture of his curls under my fingers. His steady movements, his quiet focus on unlacing my skates, pulled me back. I exhaled, shakily, and forced myself to stay in the moment. *To stay with him.* The tightness in my chest eased as I watched him, the little crease of concentration between his brows. His presence calmed the storm inside me, and the fear that had taken root faded.

He glanced up, his expression soft. "Comfortable?" he asked, a small smile tugging at his lips.

I nodded, forcing a smile in return. "Getting there."

He went back to unlacing, his fingers moving over the loops. Watching him like this, so focused, so careful, I couldn't help but think about how much I was falling for him. It was terrifying, exhilarating, and completely beyond my control.

I SAT IN THE WAITING ROOM, THE FAINT HUM OF fluorescent lights pressing in on me. The magazines on the table were brand new, but I didn't bother picking one up, particularly the one with my face on the front and the headline about me dating some big country singer. My phone was in my pocket, but I didn't reach for it to contact anyone or play games. I wanted to be here, in the moment, even if the moment sucked.

When the nurse called my name, I stood, straightened my jacket, and followed her down the hall. No Logan by my side. Just me. That was how I'd wanted it today. I had decisions to make, and this was my thing to face.

The room was the same as always. Pale walls, a desk piled with files, and Dr. Reilly sitting behind it, typing something into his computer. He looked up when I entered, offering a small smile that was more professional than warm.

"Brody," he said, gesturing for me to sit. "How have you been?"

I settled into the chair, leaning back like I wasn't carrying the weight of a bomb in my head. "I've been okay," I said. "A few headaches. Some dizziness. But nothing major."

Dr. Reilly's expression didn't change much, but I could see the subtle shift in his eyes, the way he leaned forward. "Tell me about the dizziness. When did it happen?"

I shrugged, trying to keep it casual. "It was a couple of days ago. I was on the ice, and... well, I'm not a skater. My boyfriend was spinning me around, and I got dizzy. That's all."

"How do you feel now?" he asked, his voice steady but probing.

"I'm good," I replied. "No dizziness since then. The headaches come and go, but they're not unbearable. I'm fine."

He nodded slowly; his gaze thoughtful. "Dizziness and headaches can be expected given your condition, but it's important to monitor them. They're your body's way of telling us if something is changing. How often are the headaches?"

I hesitated, then said, "Not every day. Maybe a couple of times a week. They're not migraine-level bad."

Dr. Reilly leaned back in his chair, tapping a pen against the desk. "I'd like to schedule a follow-up MRI to check up and ensure everything's stable."

"I'm already booked in for next month's check."

"We have room today."

I nodded. "I'll schedule it," I said, my voice steady. "But not today."

His eyes narrowed, but he didn't push. "Okay. But don't wait too long, Brody. Your health isn't something to put off."

"I know," I said, standing. "I'll do it soon."

I felt a strange mix of relief and dread as I left the office. I'd done this alone. I'd faced the questions, the reality of my situation, without anyone holding my hand. And I was okay. For now, at least.

TWELVE

Noah
___

THE TRIP TO ATLANTA WAS A SHORT ONE, A HOP, SKIP, AND whoop there you is, as Pops would say. It had been a week and six days since Brody and I had talked. We were now friends with benefits, which was meh. I mean, the sex was great. The man was as pushy in bed as he was on the race track, which was a massive turn-on. Nothing was more arousing than tossing two alphas into the same double bed and watching them try to get the upper hand in such a small space.

That was one of the hottest things about taking a guy to bed. You could be rough with them. Not slapping them around or anything, obviously, but with women you had to be more conscious of your strength so as not to hurt them. Also, and this was another plus in my book, there was no worry over if your lover had reached his orgasm. With women it could be tricky to be sure. There was no faking when a man came. The evidence was right there in your hand, on your stomach, or down the back of your throat. Brody and I hadn't tried anal yet. He wasn't ready. Also, it might be another power struggle to find out who bottomed. I had some vivid fantasies about Brody Vance writhing under me as I fucked him into—

"Hey, is this your dildo?"

I snapped out of my sex fantasy with a start. Blake was staring at me, a glimmer of mischief in his eye as we neared Atlanta airport.

"What?! How did that fall out?!" My throat tightened at the notion my little toy had fallen out of my carry-on. Which was secured above my head. And zippered tight. "You're an asshole."

The entire plane burst into laughter. Blake shrugged. "Sorry, rookie, but Cap said it had to be done."

Sure, okay, that was cool. Tease the rookie. I was fine with that. At least they hadn't made me sit by the bathroom. Rumor had it that our British player, Callum Ward, always got the trots when he flew. I glanced back to find Callum, a cute-as-hell ginger, sipping at a cup of what I presumed was tea as one of the two attractive flight attendants made one last pass with trash bags. Both the young ladies were very pretty, but everyone was respectful. Word was that Cap had a sister who was an FA, so if he even peeped at you getting frisky with the flight attendants, he would chew you out in front of the whole team. How this was known, I hadn't heard, but I could put two and two together.

I chuckled through my embarrassment. I knew I shouldn't have brought the little plug along, but Brody was supposed to sneak into the game after signing into his hotel. The same hotel the Railers were staying at, because why would he not. I thought we could play a little with a very small plug if he was interested. Maybe ease him into butt fun.

"Hey, seriously, it's all cool. We just like to razz the rookies," Blake confided as he sat down beside me just as the buckle seat belts announcement was made.

"It's cool, really. I was just daydreaming," I fibbed.

"About the game tomorrow?"

"Yep, totally." That was a lie. My first real pro game made me a little nervous, sure, but it was only preseason. Still, I couldn't fluff it off. I'd been extra vigilant about being on time, working hard, and controlling my numbers. I didn't want to give Coach any reason to scratch me from the roster. Every day, the numbers dwindled.

"It'll be fine. None of us are really in great form yet, and the Phantoms are looking at a massive rebuild. Their biggest threat was Cole Harrington, but he's been there four years, and he's fucking up all the ways he can. The word is that *Trick* isn't much of a treat in the locker room."

"That's not surprising. Trick's an asshole," I huffed, recalling the snub from the number-one draft pick in Vegas. "I bet he's an insufferable jerk to play with."

"He's got skills, but man, his attitude is *not* flying with the new Phantoms coach," Blake concurred. He leaned in. "Word is they're looking to get rid of him."

Trick was his own worst enemy. And not a worry of mine. He was in Atlanta, and I would only have to see him a max of two times, according to our regular season schedule. I saw enough of his father plastered all over town when he'd brought his ministry to Pittsburgh, posters about god wanting purity and all that shit. Like father, like son.

I refused to spend time thinking about Trick and, instead, pulled the conversation back to the team.

"So, is it true that Callum gets the trots whenever he flies?" I asked with a whisper as we banked to approach the airport.

"All I'm saying is to clear a path when we land," Blake replied with a wink. I figured that wink was a bullshit wink. Blake had a tendency to spin a yarn, as Grandma used to say. I missed her so bad. She had taught me her native language, as well as how to make pirozhki, little meat pies, that I loved. Sadly, they were not diabetic-friendly, so I had to avoid them or pay the price after eating one. Still, whenever I thought of her, I thought of those delicious meat pies. Pops made them on her birthday every year. His were good, but they weren't Grandma's.

We all piled onto a charter bus after landing, my thoughts on my grandmother, Brody, and the game tomorrow afternoon when I was shunted like a puck down the aisle to sit by the bathroom.

"Pardon, pardon, bloody hell, move your bag, Frosty." Callum came racing down the aisle, his hand on his lower belly. "Damn change in air pressure always riles my bowels!"

The team began to snicker as the bathroom door slammed shut. Cap strode back and handed me a bottle of Febreze.

"Rookie," he said, passing the spring-scented air freshener over as if it were a baton in a race. "You've earned this. Use it well and without delay once the door opens."

Everyone clapped. I stood, bowed, and held the air freshener lovingly.

"I shall spray with great respect for the honor this floral scented spray can bequeath," I called out so even the coaches in the front of the charter bus could hear. The guys laughed.

I chuckled too until Callum exited the toilet ten minutes later.

I WET MY LIPS FOR THE MILLIONTH TIME AS I MADE MY way to the ice for warm-ups.

Alone.

Just me. The rest of the Railers were chilling in the chute, grinning at me as I passed them. We all knew what was coming. My guts were like Callum's after a bouncy flight. I'd told myself that when this day came, I'd be cool as a penguin. I was so not cool. Excitement mingled with nerves, but as I neared the pyramid of pucks stacked by the arena staff, I could feel the flush of adrenaline. I knocked the pucks to the ice, then skated out to take my rookie lap to polite, yet mediocre, applause from the Atlanta Phantoms fans. A videographer kneeling on the ice got to his feet to follow me with the camera as I took a few shots into an empty net. The cold air on my face and in my curls felt amazing.

Then, the other teams joined me, many of the Phantoms players taking a second to wish me good luck. The Railers passed me my skid lid and thumped me on the noggin. Of course, Cole 'Trick" Harrington the Goddamn third was one of the Atlanta players to blow right by me, nose in the air.

"Douche," I muttered under my breath as he stretched off in a corner by himself.

"Totally douche canoe with tiny paddles," Nik commented at my side. I took a moment to let my nerves settle and looked around the rink. The seats weren't full, but it was preseason, and the team was struggling. The addition of Trick to the ranks had brought big excitement to the fans four years ago, but as whispers of him being reluctant to play in Atlanta began to surface, the joy was slowly dwindling. Or so the player rumor mill said. "We play hard. Big win."

I nodded with enthusiasm. My plan was to play all-out.

And so, when my third line rolled over the boards for the first time, I was more than ready. I wished my fathers were here, but both had come down with colds, and they'd opted to stay away so as not to spread the crud to me. Brody though, was out there somewhere. He'd texted right after we'd arrived at the arena to let me know he was checking into the hotel under the name Rex Racer, which had cracked me up. Only Brody would run incognito under the name of the evil racecar driver in *Speed Racer*. He had a pretty sharp sense of humor, I was learning. While I was excited to play tonight, I was just as excited to meet up with Brody in my room later.

The national anthem was sung as I rocked back and forth in the bench area, my helmet off, my attention on the tips of my skates. I wasn't thinking of anything other than hockey, which was front and center right now. When the crowd cheered, I sat, my wingers on each side, and felt a thousand butterflies burst to life inside my breast.

Atlanta won the faceoff at center ice, and they were off. Trick was truly a phenom. It was like watching tapes of Tennant when he had first come into the league. The grace on the ice, the soft hands, the innate sense of where to pass and when, or even if, to pass at all were things those generational players were born with. The downside to the greatness that was Trick was a selfish player. Unlike most of the great ones, he had zero humility, but a heaping fucking helping of ego. He knew he was good, and he liked to make sure the rest of the world also knew.

Trick was first line because, of course he was. I was third. We'd probably wouldn't meet up too often on the ice tonight, but if we did, I'd be nice. Pops and Dad were watching back in Harrisburg, my sisters on streaming services, and Babushka up in Heaven.

The game sputtered on, as most first preseason games do. The lines didn't know each other well, the goalies were rusty, and the coaches were still trying to finalize things as we fumbled around. The defense was sloppy on both sides. Offensively, I felt we had the edge, as I won all but one of fourteen faceoffs. Yeah, the stoppage was stupid high, but such was preseason.

I did get a solid shot attempt near the end of the first, but the Atlanta goalie was too fast and caught it like a line drive in his catching mitt. With five or so minutes left in the first, we took a TV time out. We all headed to the bench to rehydrate. I glanced up at the scoreboard to clock the time—as I had to piss—to find the Kiss-Kam was scanning the crowds. It moved to an old couple who waved, then smooched each other. I smiled as I rubbed at my soaking wet hair with a towel. Then, the music changed to the latest Jemima Wren song, and the camera moved, not to a couple, but to a lone figure in a Railers cap reading the program. He looked up, and I stared into Brody's eyes. The camera announced who he was even as he fumbled to find his sunglasses inside his coat pocket. The fans in his section went berserk. They flooded down to where he was seated. I watched in mild horror as he waved sheepishly at the camera, then pushed through the crowd to allow security to escort him out of his section.

"Oh man, that sucks," Blake said as the Kiss Kam swept away from Brody's back to a young couple wearing matching jerseys. "Poor guy can't even go to a hockey game in peace."

"Yeah," I said sadly.

I yanked my vision from the screen, shoved my helmet back on, and buckled my chin strap. It was the fucking pits that Brody felt he had to leave my debut game. I'd catch up with him later. We could talk. He'd be in the pits for sure. Damn man. I had always known fame came with a price, I'd grown up with famous hockey players, but this kind of madness was over the top. Why were people so fixated on a retired racer? Especially here in the States, where F1 didn't hold a candle to NASCAR's popularity, but then, he *had* dated Jemima Wren, and everyone was always up in her news.

We managed to squeak out a win against the Phantoms. The after-game interviews were done on ice, and someone who didn't know him, thought it would be fun to have Trick and me talking to the lovely Gloria Seeks, former

Olympic women's hockey player, who now worked for Atlanta.

Gloria asked Trick the big question, while sweat ran into my left eye. "So, what did you think about playing against someone who was in your draft class?"

Trick sneered. "I've been in the big show four years. He's still figuring out which way to lace his skates. Third-round pick, too—hardly worth a comparison, don't you think?"

Gloria and I gaped at Trick as he removed the headphones and skated off.

"Oh, okay, well, uhm... Noah, what did you think about your first pro game?" Gloria recovered.

"It was great. Getting the win was a nice cherry on top of a memorable night," I answered as kindly as possible, my gaze on the numbers on Trick's back. Man, what a dickhead. She asked a few more questions. I replied politely. Then, I was free to face more press in the dressing room. Once that was over, I rushed to shower, dress, and find a place to text Brody.

I had to slip into a stall in the men's room beside the skate room.

Noah: Hi. Sorry about the crowd rush. You in your room?

Ten long minutes passed. No reply, no three bouncing dots. Nothing. I was about to head out when I got my reply.

Brody: I'm heading back to Washington. Sorry, but I can't chance someone seeing me sneaking into your room. I hate this for myself and you.

"Dude, *seriously?*" I huffed to the empty bathroom. I

was tempted to throw my phone against the tiled wall, but I shoved it into my back pocket, stalked out of the bathroom, and blew into the charter bus waiting for us like a nasty thunderstorm.

The guys didn't say much as I sat in the last seat in the rear, pulled a hat on, and sulked all the way back to the hotel. Everyone could read my mood. I'd never been good at hiding my emotions, so they all mumbled goodnights as we parted in the lobby.

My room was dark when I entered it. The lights came on after I slapped the switch so hard it hurt my hand. I was pissed, hurt, and wondering what the shit I was doing right now.

I should be celebrating my first professional game tonight. I should be in the hotel bar, talking hockey, wheeling chicks, and enjoying a rare beer.

But no, I was in my room, mad as fuck.

I toed off my sneakers, peeled off my suit jacket and tie, and landed face down on the bed to scream into the void. My phone vibrated. Thinking it might be Brody calling to say his last message was a joke and he was outside my door now, I jerked it out of my back pocket, rolled to my back, and frowned at the incoming call from my fathers. Not that I didn't love talking to them but...

"Hello," I said in Swedish, then Russian, when their pale faces appeared in the box in the corner of my filthy screen. "Did you see the game?"

"Da, yes, of course. We watch with our eyes tight to the screen," Pops said, his gray eyes red and watery. "You are making good faceoff numbers. So fast! And two shots on goal. That man for Atlanta in net is drifting too far. Needs to stay in paint like tree. Plant roots."

"Stan, that's goalie talk," Dad slipped in, his blond curls coming to rest on Pops' dark head. They were such a cute couple. "You handled the puck really well. Coach Morin must be very happy with your performance. You had a plus-one tonight."

"Yeah, it was a good night." I'd not gotten an assist on our lone goal, but I'd been on the ice for it. I felt confident that Coach was pleased with my performance. "How are you two feeling? You look pale."

"Ack yes, we are palest of people. My sneezes are light now, but my nose runs like Jesse Pinkman."

I gazed at Pops in confusion.

"Stan, honey, no, not Jesse Pinkman. I think you mean Jesse Owens," Dad corrected gently before sneezing a dozen times into a wad of tissues.

"Oh yes, Jesse Pinkman is cooking drugs in motorhome with Walter White and is not running so fast unless Tuco is after him," Pops said with a nod. "You go sleep now, sweetness. I will come soon after I talk more with Noah."

"Yeah, I feel pretty crummy. Good game, son. Love you. See you next Sunday for the big Mittens birthday celebration." Dad blew me a kiss, then ambled off, sneezing and coughing as he went.

Pops turned the phone to face him as he sat back. A cat with a pink nose leapt into his lap. Dogs could be heard snuffling about in the background.

"Your da is feeling the sickness." Pops sighed as he ran

a hand over Mittens sleek white back. "I am most over it now. Just the fast nose."

"Good. I'm glad you're feeling better."

He gave me that look. The one parents give you when they know you're not really yourself, but you're trying hard to hide it.

"What is wrong?" Pops asked. I smiled a big fake smile. The urge to make something up was strong. I was a grown man now, almost twenty-two. When did running to your parents with every little problem stop? "I can feel the sadness in your face. It is long like horse, but not rubbery like horse, just long."

It all just came flowing out in a mad rush like a levee breaking. "I met this guy, and we hit it off like really fast, and then, we did shit, and then, he freaked out because he's never been with another dude before, and then, I was like fine, whatever, fuck you even though he kind of stuck with me long afterward, but then, he showed up at the practice rink, said all kinds of shit about wanting to talk and kiss more, and so did I, so we did—kiss and more, and then, we sort of had a moment, you know?—and I thought we had some sort of little breakthrough, and then, we were going to meet up here, but then, he was spotted—He's kind of famous—and then, when he got mobbed he fell back into his run-and-gun flight response, which I get because he's scared of being outed; I mean, yeah, that's scary, but he totally bolted on me, jumped on a train, and is going to his brother's or some shit, and I'm just like, am I doing the right thing, Pops?"

My father stared at me for several seconds as he ran that endless sentence through his mental translator.

"Well, son, that is big rough question. If this man is scared of coming out to world, then that is viable reason for being afraid of many consequence. Is he fellow athlete?"

"He was; he just retired."

"How old is this man?!"

"Like twenty-seven or something."

"Oh, that is very young for retiring. Is he having health problems?"

"I don't know. Not that he said. I know he has a grandfather who is a total bastard, and before you say it, I know we're supposed to respect our elders, but some old people don't deserve respect, Pops."

He sighed and ran a hand over his face. "I know this to be true so I will not chastise you for calling old person bastard. I think that maybe if you are feeling so hurt you should discuss your hurt with this man. I wish only for you to not be hurt so right now. I am thinking to find this man and shove my Stanley Cup paddle up his butthole."

"Ouch," I whispered weakly. Pops smiled a little. "No, I get it. You're right. I think he's just so damned scared about the fallout of telling the world that he's bi. Thank you for being such cool parents."

"Well, being cool is what I am most famous for. I am glad you are happy child who grows into well-round man. That is all your father and I ever wish for all of our children. To be happy and living in your truth."

"Yeah, thanks for that, too. I think I need to just get some sleep. Maybe things will look better in the morning."

"Yes, as Mama would say, the first pancake is always lumpy."

Yep, she did say that. "Thanks, Pops, it's nice to have someone to talk to about this."

"Of course, Noah, Pops is always here for you. Now, go sleep. Keep healthy. And talk to the man who is running scared. A dog in the hay will not eat it, but will sleep in the manger to keep others from eating it. That is old saying. Very old. I am not sure what matters is making here, but any dog saying is a good one. Spokoynoy nochi."

"Goodnight, Pops."

The screen went black. I stared at the ceiling for a long, long time before sending a text to Brody. I hoped it was the right thing to send.

Feeling your fears deep in my heart. See you when I get home. - N

THIRTEEN

Brody
_____

THE CODE WASN'T WORKING. I PUNCHED IT IN AGAIN, THE
worn buttons clicking under my fingers. Nothing. Just that
stubborn little beep telling me to try one more time. The
code for the gate had worked fine, but this one? Of
course not.

I sighed, dragging a hand down my face. The last thing
I wanted to do was call Logan at one in the morning to let
me in. He had to be asleep. My other option? Sleeping in
the secondhand SUV I'd bought yesterday. The same SUV
that was supposed to give me anonymity so I could slip
into the parking at the arena unnoticed and be at the game
unseen.

And look how *that* went.

So here I was, stuck outside my brother's house after
my face ended up plastered across the goddamn Jumbotron
at the hockey game in Atlanta.

I pulled out my phone and hesitated. There it was—the
message I'd ignored in the car. Hovering over it, I tapped it

open, expecting some pissed-off lecture from Noah. Instead, I got this:

Feeling your fears deep in my heart. See you when I get home. - N

What kind of nice was this? How was he such a good person? I stared at the words until they blurred, my chest tightening in a way I didn't want to name. Then, I slumped onto the cold steps outside Logan's place, dragging my jacket tighter around me. It was chilly for September, a sharp chill that crawled under my skin and made my bones ache. Fitting, really.

The door opened behind me, and I heard Logan's voice, groggy but familiar. "Brody? Are you coming in?"

I shook my head. "I might just sit here."

There was a pause, and then, the door clicked shut again. Footsteps padded across the porch, and Logan sat down next to me, wearing sweats and a jacket he'd probably grabbed on the way out. "I thought you were going to a hockey game?"

"I did," I muttered. "The Jumbotron showed my face, so I left."

"You left."

"Uh-huh."

Logan sighed. "Let's go inside and talk." Logan punched a code into the keypad by the door. "New number is 8829," he said. "Left the main gate open and had someone come in we didn't want."

I frowned. "Who?"

"Grandfather and some guy in a suit," Logan said, his voice tight. "Looking for you."

"Fuck," I muttered, my gut twisting. "Tell me you didn't tell him about my head."

"I told him fuck all, then threw the bastard out." I followed him in, kicking off my boots in the entryway as the warmth of the house seeped into my cold skin, then headed to the living room, where Logan sat in his usual chair. "What's up?"

I shrugged, running a hand through my hair. "Nothing."

Logan's expression softened, but his tone stayed firm. "Brody. Come on. You look like shit. Talk to me."

I sank onto the couch, the exhaustion hitting me all at once. "I didn't think anyone would notice me at the game," I admitted. "Guess I was wrong."

"You think?" Logan said, a hint of a smile tugging at his lips.

"I just wanted to see Noah, and we were supposed to meet up later," I said. "But the cameras found me, and I freaked out. I didn't want to answer the questions or face tomorrow's headlines. I know I'm being stupid; I mean, who the hell would care about me being at a freakin' hockey game?"

"So, you ran."

"Yeah."

"Did you talk to Noah first?"

"No."

Logan sighed, sitting down next to me. "You know, Brody, running isn't going to fix anything. You can't keep hiding from the media forever."

"I'm not," I snapped, my voice harsher than intended.

"Aren't you?" Logan said, raising an eyebrow. "You

don't want people knowing about the aneurysm, but this isn't that is it? You like Noah, but you're scared people will find out? You don't want the world to know you're bi or pan or whatever, and falling for a guy."

"Bi, and no, I'm not falling for Noah." The denial was automatic.

Logan snorted. "Your expression whenever you mention his name says otherwise."

I hesitated, glancing away. "He sees me." The words felt dangerous, too honest, but they slipped out anyway. "He told me he's happy for us to do what we're doing, but said he wouldn't wait around if I'm not out."

"He's trying to force you to come out?" Logan sounded horrified.

"No! Jeez, no. He says we'll have the friends-with-benefits thing until he wants more, which he will. And I can't give him more."

"But you like him?"

"It's only been a few weeks; I mean, we don't know each other," I stopped and stared at Logan—my brother was the only one I could tell the truth to. "That's bullshit. I know he has a big heart and is everything that would make me want to live my truth. He's snarky and positive, fighting his own battles and winning. Kind. Supportive. Sunshine."

Sexy as fuck.

Mine.

"And you want to be with him," Logan murmured.

"I don't know *how* to be with him."

The silence that followed was awful. My heart

pounded, and I dropped my gaze to the floor, unable to face Logan.

Coming out as a driver felt impossible. Motorsport—especially Formula 1—wasn't the kind of world where one could be open and out. It was a realm dominated by egos, tradition, and the relentless pressure to uphold an image of perfection. In that image, there was no space for what I desired.

I'd spent years in the paddock, and never once had I seen a current or retired driver come out. Not one. It wasn't because there weren't any. Statistically, that was impossible. It was because the culture didn't allow it. The pressure to conform, to play the role, was suffocating.

I'd lived with that for so long that I knew no different.

I swallowed hard, my throat dry, as I forced myself to keep going. "You know how it is in motorsport. There's no space for... for someone like me. And with my fucking head, I'm lost, Lo, I'm so fucking lost with what comes next."

"Brody, I know I'm not supposed to ask this," Logan said, as if he were treading on eggshells. "But... are you okay?"

I sighed, leaning back against the couch and scrubbing a hand over my face. "I had to call the doctor."

Logan's posture shifted, his focus sharpening as if a spotlight had been flipped on. "Why?"

"Dizziness. Some headaches. Nothing major." My voice sounded dismissive, even to me. "Overdid it with... things."

Twirling, dancing, living, loving.

Logan's brows knitted together, the corners of his mouth turning down. "What did the doc say?"

I hesitated, my fingers curling into the edge of the cushion beneath me. "He wants me to come in for another MRI when I can."

"Then you do that." His tone left no room for argument, his gaze steady as it pinned me in place.

"What if it's getting worse?" The words slipped out before I could stop them, low and shaky. "Just when I think I'm falling in love with Noah."

Logan blinked, startled. "'Love'?"

"Yes. No. I don't know." I waved a hand, my frustration boiling over. "What if this thing in my head steals that from me? From him? What if I can't give him a future?"

Logan sat forward, resting his elbows on his knees as he met my gaze head-on. "What if you can?"

"As a caregiver?"

"Oh, fuck you, Brody—you're not done yet. Hell, I'm still doing my job as your manager, Brody. I've got contracts for you."

"What?"

"I didn't stop after you retired. I'm not sitting here on my ass twiddling my thumbs. I have offers for sponsorships and at least three teams that want you on their roster in a technical or ambassador role if you want to return to the industry."

Hope flickered but faltered as the familiar doubts crept in, sharp and unrelenting. I dropped my gaze to the floor. "But Noah… he could be… I'm…" I didn't want to say it; I didn't want to give life to the fear that had been eating at me since my first attraction to a man. But its weight was too heavy to carry alone. "They wouldn't want me if they knew about my head or if I came out."

I glanced up at Logan, half expecting him to look away, to confirm the fears I couldn't shake. But he didn't. His expression hadn't changed. If anything, the determination in his eyes had grown stronger.

"You don't know any of that," he said. "If anyone has a problem with who you are, then they're not worth your time," he said, calm but unyielding. "But you see the doc; you get your MRI; we face whatever happens there, and then, after, there's a new career out there for you. You don't need to hide, and you sure as hell don't need to apologize for it. And even if some wouldn't go for it, others would. Times are changing, Brody. Maybe not as fast as they should, but they are. And you don't need to hide who you are to have a future. Not anymore."

Hope stirred in my chest again, fragile and uncertain, and I wanted to believe him so much. But I couldn't ignore the years of conditioning, the weight of an entire industry that thrived on image and conformity.

"Maybe," I said, my voice a whisper. "But it's not just about me. If I come out, it affects everyone around me. My team, my sponsors... you."

I felt Logan's hand on my shoulder, solid and grounding. "You don't have to carry all that alone," he said. "You've spent your whole life living for others, trying to be what they wanted. Maybe you come out and live for yourself, and maybe no one wants you, but Jesus, you're worth nearly a hundred million. You don't need the F1 circus if they don't want you."

His words hit me harder than I expected, and for a moment, all I could do was nod, swallowing past the lump in my throat. Living for myself? I wasn't sure I even knew how to do that.

But it might work out. I could have a purpose.

I could date Noah.

I could have something real for the first time.

"How would it work?"

"What?"

"The medical things, and me coming out."

Logan sat next to me on the sofa. "You want the logistics of how we'd do that from your manager's perspective or your brother's?"

"More about whether I'm honest about the aneurysm and come out, even if I am retired; it's news. Noah is... he's... I can't do that to him."

I braced myself for judgment, for Logan to flinch or pull back. Instead, his hand came down on my shoulder, solid and steady. "Maybe you need to talk to him and ask him? If it is just friends with benefits, he'll back off with any pressure, and you'll know. If he wants more, then he'll live in the spotlight. The pressure is too much, and the whole thing crumbles. But maybe it works, and it's all good, and maybe—"

"Stop doing that 'maybe thing'," I warned, and he smiled. Everything felt so hopeful, but I had a headache and...

"What about the..." I tapped my head, unable to say the word out loud.

Logan's brows furrowed, as he crossed his arms over his chest. "What about it?"

I hesitated; the words stuck in my throat. How could he not see it? How could he act like it wasn't this enormous, immovable thing between me and the rest of my life? "It changes everything, Logan," I said, my voice low.

"Why?" he shot back, his tone sharp. "Why does it have to change everything? It's a medical condition, Brody, not a death sentence. We'll get on top of this, and hell, it doesn't define you unless you let it."

"You don't get it." I shook my head, my chest tightening. I almost blurted out the whole worst-case-scenario-after-an-operation thing, but I wasn't sharing that with anyone—not even my brother. "If I started a relationship with Noah, it's not fair to keep it from him, and as soon as I tell him, it would change everything."

Logan frowned. "It doesn't have to."

I took a breath, my hands balling into fists at my sides. "He'd start looking at me like I'm fragile and might break at any second. He'd stop laughing with me the way he always does, stop arguing about stupid crap. He'd stop being himself. He'd hover. He'd worry. And then, worst of all…" I trailed off, swallowing hard.

Logan's voice softened, but it didn't lose its edge. "Worst of all, what?"

I hesitated. "He might say he wanted to be with me."

Logan blinked, confused. "And that's bad because…?"

"Because it wouldn't be real!" I snapped, my voice cracking. "What if he only said it because he felt sorry for me? Because he thought it was what I needed to hear? I couldn't handle that, Logan. I don't want to be someone's charity case, their guilt-driven responsibility."

"You're spiraling, Brody."

"I can't risk it," I shot back, my voice rising. "And I don't want to find out. If he stayed out of pity, I'd never forgive myself. And if he didn't stay—if he left because it's too much to handle—then what?"

Logan's voice was low but firm. "You can't decide what's too much for anyone. That's their choice, Brody, not yours. You're giving yourself worst-case scenarios and believing them to be true."

"Fuck. What do I do!"

"Breathe, Brody." Logan pressed a hand to my arm. "Just breathe. Okay? In. Out. Count with me. In. Out."

I listened to Logan's voice, counted my breaths, and at last, the panic began to recede.

"What do I do?"

"Talk to him."

"It's that easy?"

"Yep. Talk to him, and then, take the next step, and the next."

"Can I stay here tonight?"

"You have to ask?" Logan smirked. "You can get up early with Avery, and I can get me some Sadie smooching in, and then, we both call the doc, yeah?"

I stood, feeling determined, happy, and unhappy, a little weird and a lot stressed, and hugged Logan.

"Thank you."

"Always."

An hour later, when the house was quiet, I was still staring at my phone, my fingers hovering over the screen. I typed out a message to Noah and backspaced it so many times it was ridiculous.

Brody: I'm sorry. Can we talk when you're awake?

I pressed send and went to put my phone on the side table next to the bed, but a reply came almost instantly.

Noah: I'm here.

My chest tightened. I hesitated, then called him before I could overthink it. He answered on the second ring, his curls in disarray and his eyelids heavy with sleep. The screen barely lit his face, but I could see the faint curve of his lips as he said, "Hey."

"Hey." Silence stretched between us, thick and weighted. I cleared my throat. What did I say now?

Noah tilted his head, his smile teasing. "Is this a booty call? Because, dude, I'm wiped."

"No," I said, heat rising to my face. "Sorry, I just... It'll be a thing if I come out, particularly in the European media and the US. The whole Jemima's ex thing. Reporters will want to know everything—who I'm with, why, when, how. Our sex lives will be dragged through the press. Your dads, your sisters—it'll all come up. It'll be hell."

"Uh-huh," Noah said, unconcerned. "And?"

"It could end up destroying whatever we think we have."

"Or," Noah said, his voice steady, "it could be the best thing that ever happened."

"You're not freaking out?"

"Nope. Are you?"

"A little bit," I admitted, my voice more gentle than intended.

"Well, Brody, you should know something," Noah said, his gaze locking on mine through the screen. "I was fucking angry I didn't get to see you tonight because I miss your face when you're not around, and hell, I have feelings for you."

I swallowed hard, my chest tightening. "Okay."

"And?" Noah prompted, his eyes sparkling with challenge. "This is where you tell me how you feel."

I hesitated, words tangling in my throat. His sleepy, disheveled appearance made him all the more irresistible —his curls wild, his smile gentle, his presence magnetic. He was strong and steady, even when I wasn't. He was everything I hadn't let myself want.

"Feelings. I have them," I said.

Noah's lips curved into a small smile, his expression softening. "Feelings. Right."

I felt embarrassment creeping in as I hesitated. My words felt clumsy, too big for my mouth. "When are you home?"

"Three days," he said, his voice low and warm, carrying that sexy sleepy rasp that tugged at something deep in my chest.

"Can I be there when you get back?" The question came out quieter than I intended, as though I feared the answer.

"In my apartment?" he asked, one eyebrow lifting in amused surprise.

"No, I'll get a hotel and—" I started, but he cut me off with a laugh, the sound light and teasing.

"I was joking," he said, his smile gentle. "I'll send you the code. Make yourself at home."

"You trust me with your place?" I asked, the weight of his offer settling over me like a warm blanket. It wasn't just a casual invitation; it was something I wasn't sure I deserved but desperately wanted.

His gaze was steady. "Right now, I trust you with everything."

His words hit hard, and I couldn't speak for a moment. He didn't look away; his eyes locked on mine, and I could see the sincerity there, the strength that made him Noah. Then, he yawned, and it made me smile. He had a cute yawn.

I have it bad.

"Night, Noah," I murmured.

"Night, Brody. See you in three days."

He ended the call, and I stared at the screen for the longest time.

Three days.

That was a long-ass time to wait.

FOURTEEN

Noah

I WASN'T SURE HOW THE MARRIED PLAYERS, OR THOSE with long-term partners, did it.

I'd not seen Brody for a couple of days, yet I missed him so much it felt like a bad toothache, only in my chest. A chest ache. I rubbed idly at my sternum, the monitor hidden under my clothes, as we waited for our TSA check to return to the States from a game we'd played in Toronto. I'd not had much ice time, but the coaches were trying to get the remaining players rotated to see who was making the next round of cuts. I'd done well, considering my meager ten minutes. I'd won a few key faceoffs, taken two quality shots on goal, and blocked a slapshot aimed at our net. With my leg. The bruise on my calf was enormous, and of course, that had brought in the medical team to hover and ponder over the contusion.

Bruises are part of hockey, and I'd been iced to the gods and told to monitor my numbers over the next few days. I was to let the team doctor know if I had any other symptoms that might need medical attention, which was…

I don't know. It was good the team cared so much, but it sure would have been nice to just have a bruise be a bruise.

The discoloration was gnarly, and when I showed it off to the other Railers, it devolved into a bruise-sharing contest that ended when Coach told us to stop showing our war wounds and get the line moving. Guess he wanted to get home too. My bruise and I cleared security with no hassles although I had a joint passport, so I had to travel with my US and Swedish passports when we left the States. I had dual citizenship in both countries as I was born in Sweden but became a US citizen when I turned eighteen. Pops had been emphatic about his children being American citizens, as he proudly was. As kids, we visited Sweden many times, but Pops didn't return to Russia after bringing my siblings home. Ever. Sad but understandable.

On the short flight home, I rested, earbuds in, *Hamilton* playing as I napped on and off. The next two games would be on home ice, one against Carolina and one against Boston. I was looking forward to both. I needed to push harder now that we were getting closer to the final roster decisions. I *had* to make the team. Getting things settled with Brody was tantamount when I got back to Harrisburg.

With that goal in mind, I accepted a ride from the airport with Nic and Blake, agreed to go bowling over the weekend, then bolted—aka limped—to the lobby of my apartment. A new security guard sat behind the chrome desk, smiling at me, his teeth so white my eyes rebelled.

"Afternoon," he called as I signed in. His hair was thinning, his nose long, and his skin was pockmarked from teenage acne. He was an older guy, in his mid-fifties or so, with a paunch straining the buttons on his uniform shirt.

"Oh, Mr. Gunnarsson. Your guest is waiting for you in your apartment."

I noted his nametag. "Cool, thanks, Tim; good work keeping the tenants safe."

"That's our job. And hey, who was I to not allow Brody Vance in when he had a pass? Are you and he friends? Is this a sport thing?"

"Something like that," I fluffed off as I strolled to the mailboxes, gathered up the bills and junk, and went to the elevators. I felt bad for Brody. No matter where he went, someone was scoping him out. I got why he had fled Atlanta after that fiasco with the Kiss Kam. Hopefully, in about four minutes and counting, I could kiss his worries away.

The elevator opened on the sixth floor with a *ping*. I made my way to my door, opened it, and was met by the sexiest man in Harrisburg wearing an apron that said *Hot Rod Under Apron* and a killer smile. Pity that wasn't the extent of what he wore, but he was fully dressed. Damn it.

"You're home," he said as he produced a charcuterie board from behind his back loaded with nuts, fruits, meats, olives, and several tiny jars of seasoned mustard. "I was going to bake you a cake, but went with something better for your sugars. I looked this up on a webpage about taking care of your diabetes, and they suggested the mustard and low-carb crackers."

I smiled, dropped my bags, and walked over to him.

"This is incredible," I said, leaning over the hefty wooden slab coated with goodies to steal a kiss. He leaned into it, soft lips parting just a bit as I licked into his mouth. He tasted of spicy lunchmeats. My stomach snarled. Brody leaned back to break the kiss; his hazel eyes tender. "You're incredible. Thanks for this. I'm kind of hungry."

"Let's sit," he said, then carried the board to the living room area, placing it on the coffee table as I stepped over my bags. "You're limping."

"Meh, it's nothing. Blocked a shot in that Toronto game. Left a mark." I toed off my shoes, gimped to the sofa, and fell back into it with a sigh.

"Let me see it," he said as he sat beside me. I rolled my eyes but bent over to roll up my pant leg. "Jesus, that needs ice. Can you take some aspirin?"

"A few ibuprofen is good. Man, hey, no," I called as he shot to his feet. "Honestly, this is nothing. I don't need to be waited on."

"Yes, you do. I need to make up for... well, everything."

"Brody, you have nothing to make up for."

"Let me be gallant, okay?" The ask was genuine. I nodded. Off he went to find ice and some Advil while I snacked on meat. Mm, meat. "I'm going to snoop in your medicine cabinet," he called down the short hall. I smiled around a mouthful of salami.

"M'okay," I yelled back just as the doorbell rang. "Got it," I shouted as I rose, stole a big black olive from the tray, and went to the door. My calf did hurt, but I'd had worse. Hockey was a rough mistress. I peeked through the peephole. Pops stood on the other side, peering up and down the hallway as if expecting old Mrs. Meeler from next door to leap out and shoot a puck at his head. Well shit. I hadn't planned on introducing Brody to my family quite yet. Pops could be a lot. Still, here we were. I swallowed and opened the door. A huge box sat between me and my adoptive father.

"Ah, you are home. Good. I have need of good Swedish eyeballs and your dad is not feeling good for reading. His eyes are goopy. The doctor says he has icky virus. I did not get the icky eyes, so I think my getting a flu jab was good."

"Pops. What is this?" I tapped the cardboard box from Ikea.

He sniffled, then smiled. "Is big present for Mittens for fourth birthday. Is big white cat house with many scratching poles and special hiding box for getting away from noisy slobber dogs. We put together. I take home in truck. Hide from Mittens in the garage."

"Oh, well, Pops, I was kind of—"

"Okay, I found the ibuprofen right off and didn't poke around looking at anything else. The ice was easy to find as it was in the free—oh, hey."

Brody hit the brakes so hard it was a wonder his socks didn't smoke. He reverted from my Brody to the Brody the world saw. The transformation was astounding.

"This is awkward," I mumbled, dragging the box through the doorway to allow my father to enter. Pops strolled in, a towering man who filled the room with his presence. "Well, I guess we should do this." I shoved the box aside, pulled out my best good son smile, and introduced the two men. "Pops, this is Brody Vance."

"I am knowing him." He seemed to be a few ticks ahead of me. His gray eyes darted from Brody, in his apron holding an ice pack and a bottle of Advil, to me. "Is this the man that is making for running from you in Atlanta?"

"Uhm…" I replied. "Yes, but we're good now."

Pops' dark eyebrows tangled. "Explains just how good?" He folded his arms over his Railers Alumni Game sweatshirt, sniffled, and waited.

"Mr. Gunnarsson," Brody interjected. "I'm pleased to meet you."

"I am Lyamin, not Gunnarsson. Gunnarsson is my husband. And you are racing man who peels off away from my son leaving him feeling many bad things and being confused. Do you think to play games with my little rabbit?"

Pops was pretty damned intimidating when he wanted to be. Generally, he was a teddy bear, but if you hurt those he loved, or dared to skate into his crease, all bets were off.

"Okay, Pops, no need to be surly. Or use the rabbit name," I mumbled to the side. "We were just about to sit down and talk about things."

"I never meant to cause your son any upset, Mr. Lyamin. I'm dealing with a lot, which is no excuse whatsoever for agreeing to meet someone, then dashing off like a frightened mongrel." Brody placed the ice and ibuprofen bottle in my hand. "I'm here today to talk things over with him. I have… there are some things that we need to discuss, clear the air, and work on moving forward."

Pops took a step closer, bent down. "I am watching you most very close." Pops made the two-finger point at Brody. "My children are my most special gifts from the angels. I do not like people making them sad and unsure of themselves. You will walk a very skinny line over a pit of hungry sharks with umbrellas."

"The sharks have umbrellas?" I asked and got a dry

look from Pops, who then returned his full attention to Brody.

"The sharks have no umbrellas, the man on the wire has umbrella for making balance good. The man, who is Brody Vance, is tippy-toeing on high wire over vat. I warn you as maybe a big shark in tank, who does not have umbrella but has big teeth and knows people."

"Pops…" I limped closer. "Let's not bring up the people that you know."

"I want for him to know that I know people. I also know other things, but for him is knowing that I know the people. People who are not liking famous man with many women notched on bed posts to be making his son feel like dog shit on bottom of Gucci loafers."

"I promise that I won't harm your son's feelings ever again," Brody said. I found that vow to be a bit much at this point. I mean he might not want to hurt me again, but given where we were in terms of his acceptance of me, his sexuality, and whatever secrets he was hiding, any assurance from him was dicey, even if he meant it with all his heart. "I'm here with food and ice for his bruise to pamper him and try my best to win his trust. I do care for Noah."

"Humph," Pops said out loud. The word, not the sound, made me smile despite the tension in the room. "I am watching you close, Brody Vance."

Brody smiled and offered Pops his hand. Pops stared at it long and hard. He stared at me, and I nodded. Then, he slapped his massive hand into Brody's, making me wince. Brody grunted under his breath but shook heartily.

"Tell me of the bruise." Pops turned his attention to

me. "Did the team physician look at it? Are you icing it? Is that prosciutto on that charred cutie board?"

"Yes, yes, and yes." I led Pops around the sofa and handed him the tray. He sat, knees holding the board, and ate while Brody and I put together a cat-condo-slash-fun palace. Three hours later, and after several rounds of cussing over the complex instructions, we had Mittens' birthday present assembled.

"I am going home now to check on your father," Pops announced as his eyes flickered from me to Brody. "You two talk. Ice that bruise. I will see you both for the birthday party, yes?"

"Oh, well, I'm not sure..." Brody began, then got *the look* from Pops. "Yes. I'm just unsure what to buy for a cat with such a glorious playhouse."

"Toys with the catnip, and tuna lick sticks." Pops gave me a kiss on the top of my head, shot Brody one final two-finger motion, then carried the cat condo out of the door with one arm. I wasn't sure it would fit in the elevator, but Pops wiggled it in. "I pivot," he yelled out as the elevator door closed.

When I turned around, Brody was sitting on the floor, staring at a lone bolt lying in his palm. "I hope this isn't important."

I chuckled, limped over to where he was seated, and lowered myself to the thick carpeting.

"I think they throw in extra bits just to make people crazy." I folded his fingers over the bolt and cupped his hands. "You did so well with Pops."

"Did I? I mean, I don't think I did well at all. Every

time I looked at him, he had this icy-cold stare that made my balls shrivel."

"That's his goalie glare." I brought his hands up to my lips and placed a kiss to his knuckles. "Rumor has it that players used to feel that intense stare on them from the other end of the rink."

"I would not want to try to score on that man. Between the glare and his knowledge of people. What kind of people was he talking about?"

"No one knows. Probably best not to ask." I lowered his hand to my thigh. "Now that Mittens' condo is together, and the food is gone, I think it's time for us to talk. You want to do it here on the floor, on the sofa, or in bed?"

His gaze sizzled and sparked. "Only a fool would turn down bed." My dick grew all sorts of happy. "So, I guess I'm a huge fool because I'm choosing the sofa. You need to rest that leg with some ice while we talk."

My dick was not happy at all with that decision, even if it was the sensible one.

FIFTEEN

Brody

THREE DAYS. I'D SPENT THREE DAYS HERE, MAKING myself at home in a place that wasn't mine, surrounded by things that felt more like Noah than I could describe. I paced, restless but content, running my hands over the smooth countertops in his kitchen and the framed pictures of his family dotting the walls. His scent lingered everywhere—a mix of clean soap and something woodsy —and I couldn't escape it, not that I wanted to.

I slept in his bed, buried under the weight of a thick quilt that smelled faintly like him. I stole a pair of pajamas I'd found in his dresser, the ones with little hockey sticks printed all over them, and they were too soft, too comfortable to take off. I pulled a plain gray hockey jersey from his dryer and wore it, even though it hung loose on me.

I ordered food in, kept to myself, and avoided seeing anyone. For the first time in longer than I could remember, I felt.... safe. This place felt safe. And happy.

I was sitting on his couch, legs tucked beneath me, while Noah sat facing me in the armchair, his leg stretched out with an ice pack resting on his calf. His blond curls were disheveled, pushed back from his face with a band, and his expressive green eyes locked onto mine with a mix of curiosity and expectation. He tilted his head, his lips curling into the beginning of a smile, and I couldn't help the words that slipped out.

"How are you so perfect?"

Noah blinked, then flushed, the faintest pink creeping into his cheeks. "My sisters wouldn't say I'm perfect," he muttered, shifting a little in his seat.

"Yeah? Why not?"

He grinned, wide and wicked, his eyes sparkling with mischief. "I wasn't perfect when I drew a handlebar mustache on my sister's Tennant Rowe poster because she wouldn't let me play her stereo. She'd been obsessed with him forever—said she would marry him one day—and I thought it would be hilarious. Spoiler—it wasn't hilarious. At least, not to her. I think she cried for an hour."

I laughed, shaking my head. "Okay, maybe not perfect for them."

He shrugged, still grinning. "They mothered me even though I was a little shit."

I shook my head, unable to stop staring at him. "I still think you're perfect. For me."

The grin faltered, his expression softening. "For you?"

"Yeah," I said, my chest tightening. "And that's why this is so hard to explain."

His brows furrowed, and he straightened in his seat.

"Brody... is this us breaking up? Before we've even started?"

I leaned forward, my elbows resting on my knees. "I just called you perfect."

"That means nothing," he said, his lips pushing into a pout. "Haven't you ever seen *Les Misérables*? Darkest night, rising sun, right? Yeah, well, that's what they say right before everything goes to hell."

I let out a breathless laugh despite myself. "I don't know how you made *Les Misérables* sound so cheerful."

He grinned again, but it didn't reach his eyes. "Four years as a theater major—I've got range."

I never knew that. How did I not know he was a theater major? Did I know him at all? The thought hit me like a sucker punch. We'd only been seeing each other for... shit... how long? Days? Weeks? Time blurred when it came to Noah. It was all tangled up in moments that meant too much, and was I making this more than it was? Why was I doing this? Why was I about to entrust him with everything? My biggest secret. My panic. My shame. My anger. All of it, raw and ugly and clawing at my insides. How did I begin to explain that I'd been carrying this weight for months, alone, terrified of what it might do to me—to my future? How could I lay it all at his feet and expect him to stay?

I buried my face in my hands, my chest tight. What the hell was wrong with me? This wasn't who I was—this mess of insecurity and doubt. I was Brody Vance. I'd built a career on being fearless, taking risks, and coming out on top. But here I was, scared out of my damn mind, falling apart over the idea of letting Noah see the real me. What if he didn't have half my feelings and hated what he saw? What if I ruined everything before it had a chance to start? What if…?

I pressed the heels of my hands harder into my eyes, trying to block out the spiral of thoughts threatening to drown me. What was I thinking, letting someone like Noah in? Letting him get so close? This wasn't me. This wasn't safe. But the truth was, I didn't want to push him away. I didn't want to run. For the first time in forever, I wanted to stay, try, and trust. And it scared the hell out of me.

"Brody?" He was there, perching on the small coffee table, his hands on my knees. "Brody?"

"I'm okay, I'm…" I pointed at his chair. "Get back there and put the ice on your leg."

"You went white," he murmured, but I met his gaze, and with a huff, he returned to his chair. I couldn't do this if he was touching me.

I dropped my gaze to the floor. "Noah… I… there's something I need to tell you."

"Okay," he said, leaning forward, mirroring my posture. "Whatever it is, you can tell me. Have you been warned off coming out? Has someone found out and threatened you?"

His voice was steady as he suggested the worst he could think of at the moment, his gaze unwavering. My words stuck in my throat. I clenched my hands together, my fingers digging into my palms. He was still watching me, patient and open—everything I didn't deserve.

"I'm scared," I admitted, the words barely audible. "Not of you. Of this. Of what it might mean for us."

"'For us'?" he echoed, his voice quiet but warm.

I looked up at him, at how one wayward curl had escaped the band and rested on his forehead in a cute flick and how his eyes were soft with understanding. He was everything good that I didn't know how to hold on to. But for him, I wanted to try.

"I have an aneurysm."

The words tumbled out of my mouth before I could stop them. I hadn't planned to say it—not like this, not here, not now—but it was too late to take them back.

Noah blinked, his expression shifting from surprise to concern in a heartbeat. "You have what?"

I swallowed hard, my chest tightening as I forced myself to keep going. "An aneurysm. In my brain. It's like a weak spot in one of the blood vessels, like a balloon that could burst with too much pressure."

His lips parted, but he didn't say anything, waiting for me to explain. I hated the concerned expression in his eyes, as if he were already putting me in a bubble.

"It's small," I said, my voice sharp and defensive. "Benign. It doesn't cause me any issues. My doctor only found it because I totaled my car in Las Vegas and had to get an MRI. I wouldn't know it was there if I hadn't crashed. He warned me that I couldn't drive," I admitted, my hands clenching into fists against my thighs. "The doctors said the g-forces in racing could cause it to rupture. That's the risk. If it ruptures, it's... catastrophic. Fatal. So they told me to stop racing. They told me I couldn't get back behind the wheel. That it wasn't worth the chance."

I took a shaky breath, hating the way my voice cracked.

"That's why you retired?"

I nodded. "But it's not like it's doing anything right now. It's just… sitting there in my head and not growing. Not changing. Just… there."

Noah's brow furrowed, his fingers gripping the armrest of his chair. "But it's dangerous. Even if it's small?"

"Not if I don't do anything to trigger it," I said quickly, my voice rising. "As long as I don't do anything stupid, like strap into a Formula 1 car and push myself to the limit, it's fine. They said I could live my whole life without it being a problem."

"Brody—" Noah started.

"I know how it sounds," I said, my words rushing out as if I could outrun the weight of them. "But it's not like I'm going to drop dead tomorrow. It's just there, Noah. It's this thing I have to live with now. And yeah, it sucks, but it's not… it's not like I'm fragile or something."

Noah stared at me; his expression unreadable.

"What are you thinking?" I asked, my voice quieter, almost a whisper.

Noah didn't answer right away. Instead, he leaned forward, his elbows resting on his knees, his gaze never leaving mine. "I'm thinking… that must've been a lot to carry yourself."

I blinked, thrown off by his response. Of all the things he could've said, I hadn't expected that. Not pity, not concern—just some random thing about me.

"It's not—"

"Brody, it's okay to say it's hard. It doesn't make you weak to admit that."

His words hit me like a punch to the chest, and for a

moment, I couldn't speak because he was right. It *was* hard. And I'd spent months pretending it wasn't, pretending I could handle it all on my own. But now? Sitting here, looking at him, it felt as if it was the hardest thing in the entire fucking world, and that scared me almost as much as the aneurysm itself.

"Don't treat me like I'm breakable," I said. "I'm not dying. I'm alive, and I can still do things. I don't always need to be asked if I'm okay. I'm not scared of it, and it doesn't stop me from sleeping like a freaking baby at night, okay?"

Noah stayed silent, his gaze steady on mine as I kept going, laying out the facts. If I made it sound routine, it wouldn't feel so heavy.

"I have regular checks. There's a medic alert card in my wallet in case I'm found unconscious somewhere. And yeah, I have a DNR on file, just in case, and Logan's my proxy for everything medical. You wouldn't have to get involved in any of it. It's all taken care of."

Noah nodded, listening, and for a second, I thought I'd gotten through to him. He'd accept it for what it was, leave it alone, and maybe ask me to go, and that was something I was prepared for. But then, he rolled his eyes and leaned back, crossing his arms.

"Wow, Brody. That's so comforting," he said, his voice dripping with sarcasm. "I'm really reassured knowing you've planned for all your worst-case scenarios."

Irritation flared in my chest. "I'm being practical."

"No," Noah said, shaking his head. "You're trying to convince me and yourself that you've got this under control. But, Brody, pretending it doesn't scare the hell out of you isn't fooling me."

His words hit harder than I wanted to admit, but I couldn't let him see that. Instead, I crossed my arms and leaned back, matching his posture with a defiance I didn't really feel. "I don't need you to tell me what you think I'm thinking."

Noah blinked, his brows furrowing for a split second. I swear that sentence made sense in my head. It just… didn't come out right.

"Okay, so you have an aneurysm. Anything else?" His tone was clipped.

"No," I bit out, the tension between us thick enough to cut with a knife.

Noah stood, his jaw tight, his movements sharp as he headed toward the kitchen. "Want coffee?"

"What? No! I want to talk."

He glanced over his shoulder, his eyes flashing with something I couldn't quite name. "About what?"

"This." I tapped my temple, annoyed by how defensive I sounded.

Noah's expression hardened. He stopped in his tracks and turned to face me. "No, you don't want to talk. You want to tell me things without giving me the chance to have a reaction or feelings."

His voice wasn't loud, but each word landed like a slap. And there was anger I hadn't seen from him before, not like this.

"You've got no right to be angry!" I shouted, standing so quickly I knocked the coffee table with my knee. I followed him into the kitchen, my pulse hammering in my ears. "You have no right!"

"Yes, I do!" Noah spun to face me, his blue eyes blazing, his jaw tight, and his fists clenched at his sides. There was no mistaking the fury there now, but I thought I saw something else beneath it. Hurt. And that threw me off more than anything.

"No, you don't!" I shot back, my voice cracking under the weight of all that I felt. "I'm the one dealing with this. Not you!"

Before I could say anything else, he moved. One smooth step, and I found myself backed against the wall, his hand on my shoulder, the other cradling the back of my head to cushion the impact. My breath hitched, my heart racing as I met his gaze.

His face was so close, his expression a storm of emotions—anger, frustration, and something raw and vulnerable I wasn't prepared for. His lips parted, his breath warm, and he kissed me.

Hard.

It wasn't gentle, wasn't sweet. It was furious, desperate, the kind of kiss that demanded everything and left me gasping for air. I scrambled to hold on, gripping his shirt as my knees threatened to buckle.

When he pulled back, his chest was heaving, his eyes dark and searching mine as if looking for answers I didn't have. "I have the right to be angry," he said, his voice low and rough, "when the man I'm falling for tells me something this big and doesn't let me feel anything about it."

I stared at him, my head spinning, my heart pounding.

This wasn't how I'd expected things to go. Not even close. I didn't think he'd get angry. I didn't think he'd care enough to get angry. And that realization knocked the breath out of me more than the kiss had.

Noah's gaze softened, but the intensity was still there, simmering beneath the surface. "You think this is just about you?" he asked, quieter now but no less fierce. "It's not. You don't get to tell me how I should feel about this, Brody. You don't get to decide what's too much for me."

I opened my mouth to argue, but no words came out. Because he was right. And I hated it.

Noah's expression shifted, the sharp edges of his anger morphing into something gentler. His shoulders relaxed, and before I could process it, he stepped closer and wrapped his arms around me.

I froze at first, the tension in my body refusing to let go, but then, he pulled me in, his hand pressing the back of my neck, his other arm circling my waist. I let out a shaky breath, my chest tightening in a way I couldn't control.

I buried my face in his hair, the scent of him grounding me. His curls were silky beneath my cheek, and I leaned in closer, my nose brushing his neck, desperate for the connection, the comfort. My arms came up to hold him, as if I might fall apart if I didn't hold tight enough.

And then, somehow, there were tears. I didn't even feel them coming, but they were there, hot and unchecked, soaking into his shirt as I clung to him. My breath hitched, my shoulders shook, and Noah didn't say a word through it all.

He just held me.

He rubbed slow, soothing circles on my back, his chin

resting on my shoulder. My fingers twisted in his shirt, and I pressed my face harder into his neck as if I could somehow disappear into him and leave everything else behind. The world outside didn't matter.

I finally stepped back, swiping at my eyes with the heel of my hand. My chest still felt taut, but I managed to smile. Noah reached out and cradled my face, his palms warm against my cheeks, his thumbs brushing the dampness.

"I'm going to ask this once," Noah said, his voice steady. "Are you feeling okay?"

I nodded, still catching my breath. "Yeah."

His lips twitched into a smile, and he leaned in to kiss me—soft, lingering, and reassuring. "Okay then. Coffee?"

"Wait," I said, my heart pounding harder now than it had while I was crying. "There's something else."

Noah tilted his head, confusion flickering in his eyes. I'd already told him about the aneurysm and promised him that was all I had to say. But it wasn't true. Not entirely.

"I have seventeen million followers on my socials, a lot of them followed me when I was dating Jemima," I blurted. "I want to come out that way—nothing formal— just post and then, shut my phone off after telling my brother. Will you help me?"

He blinked, processing my words, then nodded. I turned on my heel and hurried into the front room, gesturing for him to follow. Grabbing my phone from the coffee table, I snapped a quick selfie. Then, before I could second-guess myself, I grasped Noah by the arm and tugged him into the frame.

He didn't resist as I pulled him close. His curls brushed

my cheek as I adjusted the angle, capturing the two of us together—me grinning crookedly, my eyes not too red-rimmed, and him startled but… smiling.

"It's your choice," I said, turning the phone toward him so he could see the pictures. "Which photo do I share? If it's the one of us, the media will be all over it immediately. If it's just me, the media will still be all over it—but at least we could keep us quiet for a little while longer."

Noah stared at the screen, then back at me. "Brody…"

I reached out, resting my hand over his heart. "I think I could fall in love with you, and I know that isn't fair, and I know it hasn't been long, and fuck, I didn't even know you were a theater major, but… I needed you to know."

His gaze softened, and his lips curved into the faintest smile. He took the phone from my hand, the tip of his tongue poking out of the corner of his mouth as he focused. He swiped through the pictures, his thumb hovering over the screen before finally looking back at me.

"I started to fall in love with you when you stalked me at the rink," he said, his tone teasing, but his eyes warm.

"I wasn't stalking," I protested, though the heat creeping up my neck said otherwise.

"You were," he countered, grinning.

"Okay, so maybe I was." I couldn't help the laugh that slipped out, but it was cut short as he leaned in and kissed me again.

When he pulled back, I glanced at the phone in his hand. He'd chosen the picture of us together—the one where I was wrecked, but happy, and he was like the brightest part of my world. My heart skipped a beat as he passed the phone back to me.

The caption was simple: *Boyfriends*. There were a few hashtags beneath it—something about bisexuality, love, hockey, and racing—but I didn't even read them. My thumb hovered over the screen, and I pressed send.

And just like that, I was officially out to the world.

And I had a boyfriend.

SIXTEEN

Noah

BOYFRIENDS.

That there was monumental. For Brody. For me. For the Railers. For our families.

Families. Team. Shit.

"You know," I said as my hands began a slow roam over his lean frame. "I really want to take you to bed right now."

"I like the sound of that," he replied before leaning in for a kiss. The man was temptation personified, but there were two pressing issues, and they weren't our dicks straining against our zippers. Well, they were that too, but our pricks were going to have to chill for a few minutes. "But, we should call our families. Prepare them for the media frenzy that is going to strike. I need to call my agent too, and the Railers."

He ran his fingers through my hair, combing the curls out, then watching as they bounced back. "I know that you're right, but bed sounds so much better."

"We'll get there. I promise. After our calls, we will

turn off our phones for the rest of the day and not leave my bed until tomorrow."

He smiled and nodded. I tapped his phone, slid off his lap, and sat beside him as he brought up his contacts. Within seconds, he was connected. Sitting at his side, I could only hear his side of the conversation, but things seemed chill. It soon became obvious they'd discussed this scenario beforehand, which made me happy. Knowing he had his brother always at his side eased my concern for him. His pretty eyes moved to me then.

"They want to say hello," he said, holding his phone out, then twisting his wrist to bring me into the frame. I was not ready for this, but the sight of three smiling faces erased my worry.

"Hey, so, yeah, I'm Noah," I opened with, and they all waved back.

"My dad says that you have diabetes too. Is that right?" Avery blurted out as kids do.

Her mom and dad winced. I chuckled. "Yeah, that's right, I do. I was diagnosed when I was like thirteen, so a little older than you. But it's not slowing us down, is it?"

"Nope!" She popped her *P* loudly. "I'm going to sign up for softball in the spring. I have a good arm Dad says, and Mom said I'm a slugger. I hit the ball really hard last night. It flew over our fence and into the neighbor's yard. He's really grumpy and has a big dog that my dad likes to call Hercules for some reason, but that's not the dog's name at all. His name is Brutus, and he likes to eat pickles. I know that because sometimes Brutus will sniff at a hole under our fence, and I sneak him pickles that Mom gives me in my lunches because I don't really like pickles all that much. So, I leave them in my lunch box or sometimes trade them with Connie Langley, she's my best friend in the world, for her celery. I love celery! Do you like celery?"

All the adults laughed. "As a matter of fact, I love celery," I told her as Brody beamed like a lighthouse. It was clear how much he adored his family. "Sometimes, we'll have to share some celery and talk sports."

"Yay! I would love that."

And off she ran singing about veggies. "So that's our Avery," Logan chuckled. "It's nice to meet you, Noah. And before anyone asks, yes, we got the ball back, but we had to promise the dog a gherkin for fair trade."

That broke us all up. Brody talked to his brother for a bit longer, as I made the first call I needed to make. I called my fathers. My sisters would be third. Railers would be next, but I wanted to warn them all. Kind of like those sirens that go off along coastal areas to warn about an impending tsunami. That was what these calls were—an advance emergency social media alert. Although I imagine the media already had it.

I called Dad, as he was less prone to being all "I know people" than Pops. Also, Pops would want to speak to Brody, and that wasn't what this was about. So, when Dad picked up, with a smile and rosy cheeks, I drew in a deep breath.

"Noah, this is unusual. I thought you kids would sooner die than make a call. Text or death, I think is what Margo has on one of her tees?"

"Yeah it is, but this is big. Can you get Pops into this?" I leaned back on the sofa, drew my knees up, and rubbed a nervous hand over the discoloration on my calf. Brody stayed tight to my side, his call now over.

"Sure," Dad replied warily. His parent sense had been activated. "Stan! Can you come over here, please?"

Pops arrived with a dog in his arms, Misty, a little pug mix they'd adopted about a year ago. She'd fit right in with the other five dogs and Mittens. That mansion was more like a kennel than an elite estate, but Pops loved animals, and Dad loved Pops, so it was animal central.

"Hello, Noah, we are making party plans. I am thinking fish cake," Pops exclaimed as he settled beside Dad. His dark hair, now peppered with silver, was cut short, as he liked it.

"Uhm, like fish-shaped or fish-flavored? Because I'm not sure the human guests would like fish-flavored cake."

"No, shaped. Not flavor. I am making salmon cake for Mittens. Not really cake, but salmon that I will cut into cake shape then top with candles," Pops clarified.

"Oh cool. So uhm, I have something to tell you both." I turned the phone. Brody smiled at my fathers. "Pops, you already met Brody, and I'm assuming you ran right home and told Dad all about us."

"Yes, of course. I am no for keeping secrets from my beloved," Pops stated.

"It's nice to finally meet you, sort of, Brody," Dad said, as he and Pops exchanged looks.

"I know this isn't the way you'd want to meet him, and I promise to bring him to Mittens' party for a real introduction, but for now… well, I wanted to let you know that Brody just came out on his Instagram account."

"Oh," they both said at once. "That's big news. Thank you for telling us before the poop hit the fan."

"Dad, seriously, you can say shit in front of me," I teased.

"Force of habit," Dad replied with a shrug. "Do you want me to pass this along to your sisters and aunt?"

"Yeah, please." I exhaled. "I have to call Coach next."

"Yes, you must let team know. Tell them to bring Layton in to handle the publics relations. He is old hand at making slurry into borscht. What?" Pops asked when Dad shot him an eww face. "Is old saying. Like picking sow ear and knitting it into handbag."

Brody was confused. I gave his thigh a pat. He'd learn how to decipher Pops-speak.

"Despite the slurry into soup comment, Stan's right. Layton is the VP of Communications now. He and the PR team have handled several players coming out over the years. The team will close ranks. This is going to be pretty big, Noah. Everyone knows who Brody is, and him announcing that he's gay—"

"Bi, he's bi like me," I slid in.

"Sorry, him announcing that he's bi will bring down a firestorm of press and opinions, both good and bad. Are you two sure you're ready for this?" Dad asked.

"Yeah, we're sure. It's out there now. His agent knows, and his family are behind us."

I glanced over to see Brody nodding.

"Good, good. That will make things much easier for him. Also, Brody, if you need anyone to talk to about being a queer athlete in a macho sport, Stan and I are always here. We've been through this ourselves."

"Yes," Pops stuck his face in front of the phone so now all we could see was his nose. "We are old hands at being queer. Also, I know people."

Dad tugged the phone from in front of Pops' face. "Ignore the last comment. Just know that we're here if you need us. You'll get through this fine, son. We love you."

"I love you guys, too."

The screen went blank after Pops made the dog on his lap wave goodbye.

"They're quite nice," Brody said as we took a moment to catch our breath.

"Yeah, I am really lucky." I leaned into his side, dropped my head to his shoulder, and took three cleansing exhalations. "Okay, so now, I call my agent and the team. These should be fun."

They were not fun calls. Not fun at all. My agent was super pissy about us springing this on him, which I got, but yelling out of the window of his Manhattan office wasn't going to do anything other than scare the pigeons. After his meltdown, Mike said he would meet me with the team whenever the Railers wished.

The call to Coach was less dramatic than the call to Mike, but no easier. Coach was cool about it all—he'd ridden in more than one player-induced rodeo in his time —and set things into motion for a meeting with the GM, my agent, me, and Layton Foxx as soon as it could be arranged. I suspected I might be asked to chill at home— which would cut into my playing time—and not to speak to the press—which was fine with me—until the powers that be could organize a united front. I thanked him for his understanding and hung up as the wheels in the Railers organization began clacking away behind the scenes.

"Okay, that was not the worst thing in the world," I confessed as we sat on the sofa, my hand on Brody's thigh, his arm around my shoulder. "Tomorrow morning is going to be a hellscape."

"Do we unplug from the world for the rest of today?" Brody asked with hope in his voice, his phone in his hand.

"We do." I held up my iPhone. "On the count of three. One, two, three."

We turned off both of our phones, then I slid over his thighs, settling my ass on his lap, and took his face between my hands.

"Now we make love, boyfriend," I whispered before I slanted my mouth over his.

We made out for a while, taking our time, no rushing. We had all day with zero interruptions. We peeled off each other's shirts as we tasted and nibbled, fingertips roaming at will over hard muscle. Brody's chest was firm, covered with a light furring of dark brown hair that thickened into a tempting line as it disappeared into his pants. His mouth on my throat was driving me mad in a very good way. He'd sucked a red mark onto my shoulder as I rocked back and forth, our hard dicks grinding together, our breathing ramping up with each touch and flick of a tongue over sensitive skin.

"Okay, I need more than this. Bedroom?" I asked, leaning back. His eyes were glazed with lust, his lips puffy, and his hair a mess. I loved this tousled Brody. It was so counter to the cover model racer he projected to the world.

I'd done that to him. I hoped to do more to the man before this day ended.

"Bedroom," he agreed as I slid from his lap.

He held out his hand. With a grunt I tugged him to his feet, kissed him, then led him to the bedroom. I wasn't the tidiest of men, so the bed was still rumpled from sleep. Thankfully, the cleaning lady wasn't due until tomorrow. "Can I undress you?"

"I'd be offended if you didn't," he countered with a snappy wink, but I could sense the underlying anxiety in him.

"Hey, let me put this out there right at the start. You do not have to do a damn thing that you're not comfortable with, right?" He nodded. "So, if I touch you somewhere or in a certain way that makes you twitchy say so, and we stop. No bickering, no pouting, no guilt-tripping. Consent is key for me. So, you good with me stripping you naked, then showing you a few things that I think you may like, even if they are new?"

"Strip away," he replied.

I wasted little time in freeing him from his clothing, then capturing his mouth as I pressed him back onto the bed. When we hit the mattress, he rolled us over, kissing a hot, wet path from my mouth to my nipples. He'd discovered how super sensitive they were, so he now spent stupid amounts of time nibbling on them. My hips rolled with each suck and nip, my back arching from the bed. "I love making you hot and needy," he purred, then blew over a sodden nipple. The shock zipped right to my balls.

"You're taking too damn long," I snarled, flipped him to his back and fell on his cock as if it was the first meal

I'd had in days. His hips snapped up as he moaned long and low. I loved the feel of his cockhead rubbing the back of my throat. He ran his fingers into my hair, gripping the curls as he began fucking my mouth. I groaned and hummed before popping off to tongue the slit, making sure his sight was locked on me. It was. "Now let's play."

"Okay," he huffed as I slid from between his legs, unzipped then pushed down my pants and briefs, and then, remembered the plug I'd bought was in my carry-on. "One second."

He blinked in surprise as I raced out, found my bag, then streaked back to my boyfriend. I did like the sound of that. He was resting on his elbows, cock jutting into the air, when I arrived. Those pretty eyes of his rounded when he saw the butt plug.

"If it's not your thing when we try it that's cool." I dug into the nightstand to find the lube. "I really like to play with plugs. Sometimes I leave them in when I'm home just to feel that pressure. This one vibrates. I have a blue one of the same model. That soft vibration deep inside with this nestled beside your prostate is fucking amazing. In my opinion. Your butthole may vary."

He laid back down, his thighs spread, arms resting out to the sides.

"I trust you."

I kissed his belly button as I eased myself back onto the bed. "I'll make you feel good, baby, I promise." With that I placed the plug beside him, the lube on his belly, and nestled between his legs. His cock had flagged a bit, but as soon as I had the purple head between my lips, I was rewarded with a bit of pre-cum. It took no time for his dick to stiffen again. While I sucked, I fondled his balls, rolling them, letting my fingers explore behind his sac. His breathing was rough now, his hands balling the sheets. I touched the tight furl, and he sucked in a sharp breath. I released his cock, kissed the inside of his thigh, and pulled one of his heavy nuts into my mouth.

"Jesus," he cried out while I toyed with his hole. He relaxed around the tip of my finger as it pressed the tender skin. I moved to the other ball, laving it while nudging one leg over my shoulder. "Noah, for all... Shit. That is so... I love it."

"Good," I purred as his ball slid from my lips. "I'm going to lube up a finger."

"Yeah, okay," he panted, but his attention never left my face. "I never did like having this done during medical exams."

"I feel that. But with a lover, this can be so enjoyable. We'll try it out. See if you like it. If not, we stop. If you do, we'll add the plug into play."

"Okay. Okay." He exhaled through pursed lips as I worked a line of lube around my fingers, then eased my finger back to his hole. His dick was leaking so I licked it clean, watching him watching me. He was so tight, so tense, so I let the finger rest inside him while I blew him. He loved oral sex–that much I knew–so I hollowed my cheeks and sucked like a vacuum cleaner. "Shit, fuck, yeah that is... I love that."

"Mmmm," I hummed again, pulling a guttural moan from him. I hooked my finger in more, little by little, while bobbing up and down on his cock. His body opened for me as I crooked my finger. Brody rose from the bed as if possessed. Heels digging into the mattress, hands clawing at the sheets, cock sliding so far into my mouth my nose was buried in his pubes. I loved every fucking second of it because he was experiencing this for the first time with me.

"Fuck! Fuck! Fuck!" he shouted, thighs flexing. I pulled back, letting his dick fall from my tender lips, and eased my finger out. "Shit... Noah, that was... do it again?"

"Wanna try the plug?" I asked and got a timid nod. "Any time you want to stop just say so. Yeah?"

"Yeah, just get to it because I'm a sneeze away from blowing a nut," he pant-laughed as he collapsed back onto the tangled bedding.

"Give this baby a second, and you'll be coming before you can spell sneeze," I promised as I slicked up the plug. "Legs wide, breathe, and remember that if—"

"I know. Just... insert it. God, that sounded clinical! Get it in me!" He squeezed his eyes closed while tossing an arm over his brow. I chuckled, kissed his cockhead, and rubbed the slippery end of the plug around his hole. He sucked in a breath. Kneeling between his legs, I got the prime viewing spot. With his legs spread wide, I could watch as the plug eased into him.

"I'm giving it all to you, Brody," I whispered, my voice husky as hell.

"Good, yeah, that's okay... funny, like... I don't know what but, it's okay." He wiggled his ass a little, I pressed the plug in. Then, I turned it on. "Fuck!" His shout echoed off the walls of my bedroom. I sat back on my heels to gauge where he was. His ass rose from the bed as his eyes flared wide. "Oh fuck that is… holy shit. If the… doctor did that… I'd want a prostate… check every… six months. Fuck. Oh shit, that's—"

His cock swelled.

"You like it?"

"Yes, fuck yes, Noah I'm…. that… fuck… good!"

I wriggled downward, hands pushing his legs even wider apart to make room for my shoulders.

"I'm going to make it even better," I bragged as I eased his dick down my throat again. He began to speak in tongues when I sucked his cock. I felt his orgasm pulsing out of him, each spurt coating my throat. I swallowed, grinding my dick into the bed to get some friction. He came and came and came, the tiny plug humming away. I humped the bed like a mad dog, the taste of his cum pushing me over the edge. My balls emptied onto the sheets as I moaned around his prick. He thrust upward several times, then eased out, spunk and spittle coating my lips and chin as we both collapsed into a sticky, breathless heap.

"Good… holy… hell," Brody gasped, splayed out like a limp noodle under me. I took care in removing the plug, then turning it off. I laid it on the bedding, then dropped small kisses to his spent cock before maneuvering myself up to lie beside him. His gaze fell to me as I spread myself halfway over him. "That was… there are no words."

"So did you like it?"

"Baby, that was one high-octane ride," he replied before moving over to tangle his legs with mine. "I loved it. I may never be able to walk again since my legs are now putty."

I stole a kiss. "I think my foot is in a cum puddle."

"Wow, that was romantic." He nipped playfully at my shoulder.

"Want to hear something even more romantic?"

"I'm not sure my romance meter won't burst, but go ahead and hit me with your glorious, passionate, love talk."

"Someone has to wash the plug."

He laughed so hard his eyes watered. I pulled him in close, grinning like the fool falling head over heels that I was. If only this moment could last forever…

SEVENTEEN

Brody

We managed to bypass the media, which felt like an uphill battle given the chaos my social media post had caused. They were everywhere—circling my brother's neighborhood, parked outside the gates, snapping pictures of anyone who came or went. Logan and Sadie handled the no-comment game like pros, but I could feel the weight of it, the way my mess had become theirs too. The guilt settled heavily in my chest; a constant reminder this wasn't just my burden anymore.

I'd hired private security to patrol their house and keep an eye on Noah, though he didn't know about that part. It wasn't as if I was following him; I couldn't risk something happening to him because of me. The thought was enough to keep the guilt at bay—just barely.

Getting to the doctor's office was a covert operation in itself. We slipped through a back entrance, Logan leading the way while I kept my head down. The clinic was quiet, the fluorescent lights casting a sterile glow over the empty waiting area.

Dr. Reilly met us in his office, his face a practiced mask of calm professionalism. He gestured for us to sit, and I sank into the chair, my heart pounding. Logan settled beside me, his presence steady, but it didn't stop the tension from coiling tighter with every passing second.

"I've reviewed the MRI results," Dr. Reilly began, his tone measured. "And as you thought, the headaches and dizziness are due to a change."

My stomach dropped. "What kind of change?"

He folded his hands on the desk, his gaze steady but serious. "The aneurysm has grown. It's still small, but the growth indicates increased pressure in the vessel wall. At this point, we need to consider surgical intervention."

The words hit me like a freight train—surgical intervention. My chest tightened, my breath shallow as the room seemed to shrink around me. "'Surgical intervention'," I echoed, my voice barely above a whisper.

Dr. Reilly nodded. "Yes. The good news is that it's operable, and the prognosis is positive. However, I won't sugarcoat this—there are risks. It's brain surgery, Brody. As I explained before, complications are rare but can include issues with memory, motor skills, or speech," he explained. "We'll take every precaution to minimize those risks, but you must be prepared for the possibility."

Logan leaned forward, his tone firm but calm. "And the good news? What's the best-case scenario?"

Dr. Reilly's expression softened. "The optimal outcome is that we successfully repair the aneurysm, and Brody fully recovers with no long-term effects."

Logan's hand landed on my arm, a steadying weight. "Then, that's what we'll focus on."

I couldn't share his optimism. My thoughts were stuck on the words *"brain surgery"* and *"risks,"* circling endlessly until they drowned out everything else. I stared at the desk, gripping the edge of the chair as if it could anchor me. I felt as out of control as when I'd lost traction at a hundred and ninety miles per hour during qualifying in Monaco, the car spinning out in the rain while I fought to regain control. Like then, as other cars headed straight for me, I could do nothing but brace for impact and hope the damage wouldn't be catastrophic.

Dr. Reilly cleared his throat, pulling my attention back to him. "I understand this is a lot to take in. I'll give you a couple of days to process, but we must schedule the surgery soon. The longer we wait, the greater the risk of rupture."

I nodded, unable to trust my voice. Logan spoke for both of us, thanking the doctor and promising to follow up as we left. My legs felt as if they were moving on autopilot, each step toward the car heavier than the last.

I collapsed into the passenger seat, staring out of the window. My hands trembled, and I clenched them into fists to stop the shaking.

Logan started the engine, his grip tight on the steering wheel. "We're going to get through this," he said, glancing at me. "You're not alone in this, Brody. We've got a plan, and we'll make it work."

"What if it doesn't?" The words slipped out before I could stop them, raw and desperate.

Logan's jaw tightened, but his tone didn't waver. "Then we'll figure it out. You've got Noah now. You have a future and don't get to give up, little brother. Not on this, and not on yourself."

I turned my head, meeting his steady gaze. I wanted to believe him, to cling to the hope in his voice, but the fear was too loud, drowning out everything else. For now, I could only nod and hope he was right.

I owed it to Noah to tell him. No more delays, no more half-truths. He deserved to know what was happening, to understand the risks and the reality of being with me post-operation. But even as I thought about it, my chest tightened again. How could I tell him without making him see me as fragile or broken?

"Have you thought about telling anyone else?"

I was horrified. "Not our fucking grandfather, he'd monetize it somehow, make me a huge pity party, and—"

"I meant Jemima."

"We message," I hedged.

"So you've told her about the aneurysm?"

"No. She knows I'm bi though."

He shot me a pointed look. "Call her before the media gets hold of it."

The car was silent except for the soft hum of the engine, and I hesitated, staring at the name on my screen. *Jemima.* It had been months since we'd last talked, but she was still one of the few people in my life who *actually* knew me—who'd seen me at my best and worst and never judged me for either.

I'd lost track of where in the world she was, but I hit *call,* half hoping she'd answer and half hoping I could leave a message. The line rang once, twice, and then—

"Well, if it isn't my favorite ex."

Her voice was the same as ever, light and teasing, but I could hear the undercurrent of surprise. I never *called* out of the blue; we always messaged.

"Hey, J," I said, exhaling. "You got a minute?"

"For you? Always. What's up?"

I swallowed. "I need to tell you something. And I don't want you to hear it from the media."

Her breath hitched. "What is it?"

I forced the words out. "I have an aneurysm. In my brain. They found it after my crash in Vegas."

Silence. Long enough that I checked the screen to make sure the call hadn't dropped.

Then, her voice, small and broken. "Oh my God, Brody."

I closed my eyes. "I'm okay. It's—small. Stable, for now. But I need surgery."

"When?"

"Soon."

A shaky breath. Another pause, and then, in true Jemima fashion, she sniffed, pulled herself together, and squared her shoulders, even if I couldn't see it. "Well. Chin up, Vance. You'll get through surgery, and when you do, we're celebrating. I'll visit when I'm back from Europe. And if you need me before that… you get that sexy brother of yours to call me."

Logan snorted under his breath, and I huffed a quiet laugh, the tension in my chest easing just a fraction. "You don't have to—"

"Shut up, I want to." Her voice softened. "I love you, B."

I swallowed past the lump in my throat. "Love you too, J."

There was nothing romantic in the words. Just history. Just understanding. Just us.

She cleared her throat. "You want me to get ahead of this if it leaks?"

"No comment always works for me."

She chuckled. "Figured as much. But you know where to find me if you change your mind."

"I do."

A pause, then, "Take care of yourself, Brody. Get Logan to… get him to… tell me how you are, okay?"

I glanced at Logan, who nodded. "He will." I ended the call, staring at the phone briefly before setting it down. The car was still silent, but the world outside kept moving.

LOGAN DROPPED ME AT NOAH'S FAMILY'S HOUSE. ERIK, who hadn't eyed me as though I was a threat, had given me all the codes: the gate, the internal gate, and the door. They took security seriously, and for that, I was grateful. They didn't know about the extra layer of protection I'd added with the private security team, but maybe I should be honest.

I steeled myself for the dreaded conversation when I knocked on the door. But before I could say a word, the door flew open and Noah was there, grinning from ear to ear.

"I made the team!" he shouted, and before I could react, he jumped at me, wrapping me in a tight hug and swinging me around as if I weighed nothing. "I made the team!"

I clung to him out of instinct, laughing despite myself. "Noah, that's amazing!"

"Come in! We're celebrating!" he said, dragging me inside with an energy that lit up the entire house.

The kitchen smelled of spices and roasting meat, a warm mix of dill, garlic, and something buttery that clung to the air. Stan was at the stove, fussing over what looked like an enormous pot of stew or something, his brow furrowed with concentration. Erik leaned against the counter, nursing a beer. His posture was relaxed despite the buzz of activity around him, and he lifted his bottle in a hello. The counter was loaded with platters of food: stuffed cabbage rolls, blinis stacked high, bowls of sour cream, and tiny pickles—a feast fit for a celebration, all with a distinct Russian flair.

"Thirty minutes," Stan warned, not even glancing up as Noah tugged me past and up the stairs.

Noah led me into the room he was staying in, and the first thing I noticed was how lived-in it felt; it must have been his childhood room. Posters of hockey players I didn't recognize covered the walls, trophies lined a shelf, and a pile of plushies sat in the corner of the bed. It wasn't what I expected, but it was so undeniably Noah it made me smile.

He turned to me, his eyes still shining with excitement, and before I could say anything, he threw his arms around me. We hugged, his warmth seeping into me as I held on.

When he pulled back, his grin hadn't dimmed. "Can

you believe it? I made the team! Fourth line for now, but I'm there!"

I kissed him then, quick and light, because he was so high on the moment, and I couldn't bring myself to dim that light. Not today. "I'm proud of you, Noah. You earned this."

His cheeks flushed, and he laughed, dragging a hand through his curls. "Thanks. It's… it's just huge, you know? I can't wait for you to see me play for real, sitting in the stands or a box. Probably a box, right? And it won't matter if you get spotted because you're with me, I'm with you, and I love you!"

"I love you, too, and I'll be at every game I can be," I promised, though the words felt heavy with everything I hadn't told him yet. Tomorrow, I thought. Tomorrow, I'd tell him. But not today. Today was his moment, and I wouldn't take that away from him.

That's my excuse, and it's valid. Right?

I'm not a coward.

I'm not.

Dinner was exactly what I needed, even if I hadn't known it before. The atmosphere in the kitchen was light and celebratory, Stan explaining every dish in detail with pride as he served us. Erik sat on the counter; his beer forgotten in his hand as he watched his family with a quiet pride I envied more than I cared to admit. Every laugh, every joke, every shared memory filled the room with a warmth I hadn't felt in years.

Halfway through, there was a knock at the door. Noah shot me a look of excitement as he jumped up to answer it, and a moment later, he returned with two men. One of them I recognized from the posters on Noah's walls—Tennant Rowe—a hockey player, or a former one at least. The other was older, blond, with an air of calm authority and a smile that hinted he didn't miss much.

"Noah!" Tennant's voice was loud, his grin infectious as he pulled Noah into a bear hug. "You did it, kid! I knew you would!"

The other man, whom Noah introduced as Jared, clapped Noah on the back with a quieter, "Proud of you, Noah. Couldn't be happier."

And then, Tennant turned to me. "And you must be Brody." His handshake was firm, his expression open and curious. "Noah's been messaging me about you. A lot."

"Has he?" I glanced at Noah, and he flushed, though he didn't deny it.

"Uncle Ten!" Noah groaned.

Tennant laughed, his energy filling the room as he sat at the table. "Let me tell you, this kid right here"—he pointed at Noah—"has been a firecracker since day one. I remember he insisted on carrying tiny hockey sticks for every occasion when he was little. I mean, everywhere. Grocery store? Tiny hockey stick. Bath. It's a tiny hockey stick with a sponge. Weddings? It's a tiny hockey stick to dig into the cake. I had one custom-made for him to use in the pool because I couldn't get over how cute it was."

"Still have it," Noah admitted, his voice soft but proud. "It's in my room, along with all the other stuff I have of yours that I can sell on eBay."

Ten clutched his chest. "Ouch!"

The banter had everyone laughing. Ten and Jared were easy to be around, and their excitement for Noah was infectious. The night included stories from when Noah was a kid, from when his dads and Ten played for the Railers, or when Jared was a defensive coach, about how he and Ten paved the way for others. However, neither of them would admit they'd done anything remarkable.

"Did you always want to play hockey?" I asked during a lull in the conversation. I'd never thought to ask him before, I kind of assumed that, like me, family legacy dictated what he'd become.

I hadn't seen my grandfather since that day I left his house. Still, he hadn't given up—he kept sending me emails about promotional opportunities countered with how fucking disappointed he was in me letting him down. He called me a coward so many times that I almost believed it.

At least, I would have if I wasn't with Noah.

Somehow, being with Noah—loving Noah—made my grandfather's controlling ways and bitterness less than nothing.

"Little Rabbit always wanted to be hockey player."

"Apart from when he wanted to be a rodeo clown," Erik reminded him. "Or a chimney sweep."

"Sweeping the chimney he sees in Poppins movie. I am not sure when he sees clown in rodeo, but I know for good he could be anything he wants to be."

I reached for Noah's hand under the table, and he squeezed mine, his smile warm and steady. At that moment, everything felt right. The worries, the fears, the weight I'd been carrying were still there, but for now, they didn't matter. All that mattered was this. Him. Us.

Tonight.

After we'd moved to the large living room, I cuddled into Noah's side on the vast sectional, and Ten dozed off, his head resting on Jared's shoulder as the room quieted. It was Stan who broke the peaceful silence, his deep, accented voice cutting through the soft hum of conversation.

"How is head?" Stan asked, his words blunt but laced with concern.

I snapped to attention, my chest tightening. Were they talking about me? Had Noah told them? My gaze flickered to him, looking down at me, searching for answers in his expression. But Noah shook his head, his eyes steady on mine. He hadn't said anything.

Instead, he cleared his throat, his voice steady as he answered. "He's talking about Ten."

Stan nodded, his eyes warm as they landed on Tennant, still dozing. "When he was young man, he have big hate with other snake player. Very bad man. Evil. One game, Ten fall to ice with big crash. Very bad. Blood everywhere. No speaking from Ten for many days. Bad brain for pudding inside skull."

Jared's hand settled on Tennant's back, his touch light but grounding. "It was a bad fall," he said. "Traumatic brain injury. There was a lot of swelling, and for a while, we didn't know if he'd fully recover."

"Bad times," Stan whispered.

"The good news is," Jared added, his tone brightening, "that aside from headaches and occasional confusion, Ten is happy, coaching peewee hockey, and enjoying retirement."

The tension in my chest eased, replaced by a strange

mixture of relief and an unnamed feeling. Watching how Jared's hand rested on Tennant and the way Stan's eyes softened when he looked at them, I felt a pang of something reminiscent of envy.

I cuddled closer to Noah, needing the contact. He squeezed back, his thumb brushing over my knuckles in a way that made my chest ache with something warm and unfamiliar.

"Good," Stan said, his lips curving into a small smile. "He is strong. Like my Little Rabbit."

Noah ducked his head, a faint flush creeping up his neck. "Thanks, Pops."

I stared up at my Noah, then *really* looked at him. His blond curls were messy, his eyes bright despite the late hour, and a smile tugged at his lips. Perfect. He was perfect.

"Can we talk?" I whispered, and Noah smiled down at me, waggling his eyebrows.

"Talk, huh?" His smile faltered. He was teasing but must have noticed something in my expression. "Heading to bed!" His loud announcement woke Ten, who blinked at us and smiled.

"Already?" Ten said, with a pout, then a grin.

"Go back to sleep, babe," Jared laughed.

"Is early still. Lightweights," Stan teased, his thick accent wrapping around the word as he glanced at Noah and me. "Shameful manly ways. It's only ten o'clock. Back in day, we party until sunrise, then beat Boston seven-one!"

Noah shot him a grin, his curls bouncing as he turned to grab my hand. "Some of us have practice tomorrow at nine," he said, his voice full of mock seriousness. "Can't all be retired legends like you, P!"

"Excuses," Stan muttered, but his smile betrayed the pride in his eyes as he watched Noah pull me toward the stairs.

"Night, everyone!"

The four retired guys sketched waves at us, and I waved back.

"Come on," Noah murmured, his hand warm and firm around mine. "Let's get some sleep."

We climbed the stairs, the sounds of the party growing fainter with every step. My heart was pounding, and it wasn't from the climb. I knew what I had to say and couldn't put it off. But the weight of the words made my chest tight, my thoughts swirling with what-ifs and worst-case scenarios.

Noah tugged me into his childhood room. As soon as the door was shut on us, he turned to me, his expression softening as he caught the look on my face. "What's wrong?" he asked, his voice low and steady.

I hesitated, the words catching in my throat. "I need to say something," I whispered, the vulnerability in my voice making me cringe.

He nodded, stepping closer and brushing his thumb over my hand. "What's going on?"

I waited for him to ask if I was okay, but he didn't, which threw me a little. I took a deep breath, forcing myself to meet his gaze. "I went to the doctor today."

His brows furrowed, concern flashing in his eyes. "Okay," he said. "You're scaring me a little."

"I don't mean to," I said, running a hand through my

hair. "The doctor wants to operate. It's... it's gotten bigger."

Noah froze, the weight of my words hanging between us. His hand tightened around mine, his expression shifting from shock to worry. "'Bigger'?" he repeated, his voice barely above a whisper.

I nodded, swallowing hard. "Yeah. It's not... it's not an emergency yet, but they don't want to wait. There are risks if we don't do it soon, and risks if we do it, and... fuck. So many risks."

He stared at me for a long moment, his jaw tightening. "What kind of risks are we talking about?"

"The usual," I said, trying to keep my tone light even as my chest tightened. "Memory, motor skills, speech. You know, stuff you don't want to mess with."

"Brody," he said, his voice breaking on my name. He pulled me into a hug, his arms wrapping around me. I buried my face in his neck, clinging to him as the tension I'd been holding onto for days finally began to ease.

"I'm sorry," I murmured, my voice muffled against his skin. "I didn't want to ruin tonight, but I promised I'd be honest with you, and I can't keep it from you anymore."

He held me tighter, stroking the back of my head. "Don't apologize," he said. "You don't have to apologize for this. For any of it."

"I'm sorry you fell in love with someone who—"

"Stop right there," Noah warned, and I buried my face in his neck again. "When?"

"The operation?"

"Yeah."

"Soon."

"How soon?"

"As soon as I decide to do it. A week, a month, a year?" I shrugged because it would be less than that if I decided to proceed. There was no point in delaying the inevitable; however much I wanted to stay in this moment with Noah.

"But the doc says you need it, now? Tomorrow? The day after? Is it an emergency? Should we go now?"

"Not tonight, but soon."

We stood there for what felt like an eternity, the world outside fading away until it was just the two of us. Finally, he pulled back enough to meet my gaze, his hands still on my shoulders.

"Okay, it happens, and when you wake up, I'll be there. I won't let anything happen to you," he said, his voice firm and unwavering. "I just found you, Brody. I'm not losing you now."

The sincerity in his words broke something inside me, and I nodded, unable to find the words to respond. He kissed me, slow and soft, as though he was trying to pour all his love and determination into that moment.

When he pulled back, he rested his forehead against mine, his breath warm on my skin. "We'll get through this," he said. "Together."

I nodded again, a small, tentative smile breaking through the weight in my chest. "Together."

EIGHTEEN

Noah

"TOGETHER MY ASS," I SNARLED AS I TAPED UP MY STICK.
Brody had put his foot down, the lead one that was heavy
as hell, and said I needed to come to practice instead of
going with him for all the pre-op shit followed by a visit
with the neurosurgeon who was doing the operation. "You
need to stay focused on your hockey career, Noah," I
mimicked him as I wrapped black tape in a precise, but
pissy, manner. "You're on the team now, but they could
send you down if you get sidetracked, Noah." Nik jogged
by in his cup with a red wig on. No clue. And I was too
angry to question. "Go to the rink. Concentrate on hockey.
Stay away from social media blah, blah, blah."

"So is talking to inanimate objects like a hereditary
thing?" Blake asked as he sat beside me clad in hockey
pants, socks, and nothing else. I glared at him as I went to
work on taping stick number four. Did I need this many
sticks ready for practice? Nope. But if I didn't do
something constructive with my hands I'd be punching

walls in sheer frustration and worry. "Your dad talked to his pipes all the time."

"Pops is my father by marriage, not blood, and you can't inherit something via mental congress, asshole," I snarled.

Blake, as expected, drew back as if I'd slapped him. "Dude, chill the hell out. So sorry I don't know your genetic markers and all that. Christ. I was just trying to make some pleasant conversation, maybe get you to smile."

My sight flew from my stick to my linemate. "Here's a thought, maybe you should mind your own business. Maybe, I don't want someone coming over here talking shit about my family when they don't even know that Stan is my adoptive father. Maybe you should find someone else to make smile."

He stared at me for a long-ass moment, nodded, got to his stocking feet, and walked off. The dressing room was dead silent. Like mausoleum-still. I must have spoken louder than I'd realized. Damn it. Shit.

And now, here came Cap wearing his official captain face.

"We have a situation that I'm not aware of brewing?" Cap asked, standing in front of me like a sequoia, arms crossed over his wide chest. I shook my head. He didn't leave. I returned to taping my stick. "Well, Gunny, that sounded like a situation. Is there a reason that you just tore your linemate's head off that you would like to discuss privately?"

I chucked my stick to the floor, shot to my bare feet, and glowered up at Jack. "I have two metric tons of shit to carry around today, okay? The press is all over me like syrup on a pancake whenever I leave the house, my boyfriend is facing some pretty big medical drama, and my head feels like someone stuffed it full of cotton batting. Does that answer your questions, Cap, or do you want more intimate fucking details? Do you want to know what I ate for breakfast, when I last took a shit, and what Brody told me was—"

He place a hand on my shoulder. I flung it off, my vision red, and took a swing. At my fucking captain. You could have heard a pin drop in that dressing room. Cap caught my shaky right fist, the roundhouse a mile off, and held onto my hand tightly.

"You and me are taking five," he told me in a low, growling voice that brooked no further bullshit. He tore his gaze from me to whip the dumbfounded Railers gawking at us with his glare. "You chuckleheads get on the ice. Tell Coach Gunny and I are having an informal peer meeting and will join the rest of the team on the ice shortly."

Fifteen men murmured a "yes, Cap.".".

"This way." Cap released my hand.

Head hanging, tail tucked, I trudged along after Jack, knowing I was going to get my ass chewed, and rightfully so. He opened the door to the skate-sharpening room.

Casper, one of the equipment managers, glanced up from relacing a skate. "Hey, guys, you need some skate work?"

"Could we get this space for five minutes, Casper?" Jack asked. Casper looked at the mound of skates requiring attention. "Trust me, it will only be five minutes. Maybe less. Go get some coffee and a donut in the film room."

"Oh-kay," Casper said, leaving us to it. Cap closed the door, turned, and studied me for a good fifteen seconds.

"I didn't mean to take a swing at you," I said meekly, his scrutiny making me feel just as I had when I was six years old and had called my Nana a nasty witch. Pops had come down on me hard that day. "I was caught up in some shit and… it was all personal. I'm sorry."

He drew in a breath, his expression stony. "So here it is, you take this for what it's worth. All of us on the team are fully aware that you're carrying a crazy amount of stress for a rookie. Your relationship is everywhere. I can't visit any social media site without seeing you, Brody, or Jemima. I get it. It's stupid stressful, which is probably affecting your sugar levels. Am I correct in that stress will make your numbers go flaky?"

"Yes, sir, yes, that's right." Gods, lying was the fucking worst.

"As I thought. So, what we're going to do, rookie, is this. You're going to skip this skate due to some issues with your diabetes. Nothing severe, but you're feeling out of sorts. You're going to go home, rest, and get your head pulled out of your asshole. Because, and I'm saying this with all the love that I have for a tiny little newbie who looks up to me, if you ever take a swing at me again, I will drop you like a stone, son of a HHOF goalie or not. Do we understand each other, Gunny?"

"Yes, sir, yes, I understand one hundred percent," I replied, keeping my spine stiff so he didn't see me wilting outside as I was inside. "Thank you for covering for my… my—"

"Assholery works, rookie. Now, go talk to Doc." With

that he gave me one long, firm stare before exiting the room. I stood there panting, my heart thundering.

"Noah, you are a fucking idiot," I grumbled as I slunk off, passing Casper who watched me skulking past him like a whipped potato, to find the team physician.

After a thorough check-up and a thousand questions about mental health, he made the call. I was put on the injured reserve list. Which sucked big time. I would be able to return to active play in seven days, which, thank all the hockey gods, got me on the ice for the season opener against Washington, but it still blew.

"So I'm not being sent down?" I asked Doc for the tenth time as I slid from the exam table.

"No, not for this, but I am going to note that your diabetes needs a firmer regime implemented when you return." He gave me that I'm-very-serious-here doctor stare.

"Cool, yeah, I'll work harder on it. And the stress. I promise. I'll take up yoga."

I bolted before he could change his mind.

When I returned to the locker room, it was empty. I undressed in silence, flung my gear into my cubicle, and pulled on my street clothes.

I took a second to go to the whiteboard on the wall. Using the sleeve of my Railers hoodie, I wiped off the *X*'s and *O*'s to write *SORRY FOR BEING A SPANK– GUNNY,* under which, I drew a big old dick with an arrow leading from Gunny to the penis.

On the way home, I stopped to grab a milkshake at the ice cream shop and sat in the car staring at it, knowing I would pay for the indulgence. I drove home, headed for the back entrance, as the press milled around outside the front doors, and rode up to my floor sucking on my shake. Mm, mint chocolate. A chip got stuck in the straw, so I had to suck super hard as I padded down the hall.

As I fumbled with my keys, the one bright spark of the day was knowing that I could now go with Brody to the doctor. We'd have to go incognito to avoid the crush of nosy paparazzi, but at least we'd be hand-in-hand.

I threw the door open, stepped inside while looking for Brody, and tripped over a suitcase. I nearly dropped my shake as I shouted in surprise. Brody came jogging out of the bathroom, shaving cream on his cheeks, and stared at me as if Lucifer had just strolled into the apartment.

"Noah," he coughed out, wiping at his face with the hand towel resting on his shoulder.

I stared at the suitcase to make sure I wasn't hallucinating from the sugar rush. I tapped it with the toe of my sneaker. Nope, it was no visual disturbance. It was a packed bag.

I glanced up from the bag to him. "You weren't going to talk to the doctor at all, were you? You're going to the hospital today. Fucking hell, Brody! Were you even going to tell me? I thought we were doing this together!"

"I didn't want to say goodbye," he whispered, shamed, as he should fucking be.

"So you just were going to sneak off, go under the knife, and not let me know?! Fuck, what kind of miserable snake shit is that? I can't *believe* you!"

I slammed my shake to the coffee table. The cup crinkled on impact, melted ice cream oozing out of the straw as I glared at the shake.

"Noah…"

I drew in a wobbly breath, sat down with a huff, and buried my face in my hands.

"Today is officially the worst day in a string of miserable days," I said into my palms.

"I was going to have Logan call you when it was done," he said as he sat beside me on the sofa. "He would have filled you in if things went well."

I jerked my head from my hands to power glare at him. "And if things went wrong?"

"Then, I wouldn't have had to say goodbye."

"Coward," I snarled, tears forming. I swiped at my eyes with the back of my hands. "How dare you make that decision for me?! We're boyfriends, Brody. Do you know what that means?!"

"No, I honestly don't. I have no idea how to do this relationship-with-a-man thing." His dark eyes were glued to me, dewy as mine were. "I thought I could spare you the grief of looking at my corpse."

"Maybe I want to see your corpse!" I fired back, then realized how awful that sounded. His eyes rounded. "Not like that. Shit, I am all over the place today. You're making me nuts, Brody. Truly and astronomically bonkers! I yelled at Blake, took a swing at Cap, and was put on the IR list for a week to get my 'shit together.' Then I came home to find out that my supposed boyfriend was going to sneak off to get his brain operated on without telling me. Fucking fuck of all the fucks!"

I grabbed my shake, tore the lid off, and downed the rest of the warm shake in two shuddering gulps. Who needed booze when sugar would get a man buzzing?

"Noah, why the hell are you drinking a milkshake? Your sugar is going to—"

"Nope!" I poked a finger at his noble nose. "Fuck off," I snarled, then burped. "Maybe I'll go find some candy to chase down the ice cream. Then, I'll hide somewhere and go into a coma, but you won't know because we didn't love each other enough to be totally fucking honest with each other."

He stared at me as if I'd slapped him. "Yeah, okay, I get it. I get it."

"Do you? Do you really? Because I'm really mad at you for this stunt. If you ever do something this selfish again, I will... I'll... I don't know what I'll do, but it will be stupid. Just like that." I waved a quaking hand at his suitcase.

"No, you could never match me for stupid," he whispered.

"No shit," I panted, wrung out and on the verge of a crying jag. Also, I was feeling crappy now—stupid sugar. Sometimes, I could live with my illness, and other times, I wanted to be normal. Boyfriend does something stupid? Eat a pint of ice cream, then watch a chick flick like the rest of the world. No, not Noah Gunnarsson. I needed to piss. Again. Not a great sign. "I need insulin."

He went pale. "What can I do?"

I looked right at him. "You can stop trying to protect me. We do this together. All of it. The good, the bad, and the fucking ugly." He nodded. "Now kiss me, then let me get my sugar down, then we'll go to the hospital. Together."

His lips touched mine, sweetly, shyly. I let my head

drop to his shoulder for a moment, then I did what my body needed. I rested after the spike, while he returned to shaving. When I was feeling better, we left my apartment. Together.

With security tight to us, we sneaky-snuck out of the janitor's exit to a waiting car.

We rode to the hospital in DC. Together.

We were rushed into yet another side door. Together.

And when we were in his private room, we stood at the window and stared out at the Washington Monument in the distance.

Together.

I could feel his anxiety from ten feet away. He didn't pace or chew his lip; he kind of vibrated with worry. Nurses came and went as he changed into funky little grippy socks and one of those sexy-as-hell hospital gowns. When I was helping him tie the strings on the back of his gown, the door to his room opened again.

"That's certainly a look, B," a woman's voice said. I glanced over his shoulder to see Jemima Wren standing just inside the doorway, bracketed by two behemoth bodyguards. She tossed her ballcap and shades to the bed as I gawked like a dodo. "Your knees are still super cute."

"Jem, why are you here?" Brody asked as the slim olive-skinned woman embraced him while her dark eyes met mine. "When we talked yesterday, you said you were in Canada recording a new album."

"I was. I'm here to wish you well. Course, I had to annoy the hell out of Logan to get the truth about where and when you were going under the knife." She pecked his cheek, and then, smiled at me. I'm glad to hear it wasn't just me he had been hiding this from. "And is this your personal nurse? He's adorable. And those curls! But I'm not sure dirty Nikes are exactly sterile."

"I'm Noah." I reached over Brody's shoulder to shake her hand. "I'm his boyfriend."

"I know." She winked. "The whole world knows." She smiled down at Brody. "I'm so proud of you, B, for coming out boldly. That was a monster fuck-you to the uptight racing world and your asshole grandfather."

"I'm not so sure it was the fuck-you that you think it was, but it felt right." He glanced back at me, grinning at the pop superstar in baggy jeans, ratty sneakers, and a blue tee with a plump penguin on the front. "We're together."

I hugged him from behind. Hard. Finally. He *finally* got it. Jointly. With each other. That was the only way to face down the hard shit that life flung at you. With the person you love at your side. My fathers taught me that. Nothing could knock you down if you faced it with love.

Together.

NINETEEN

Brody

DARKNESS EBBED AND FLOWED AROUND ME, A HEAVY FOG as I fought my way back to the surface. My eyelids felt weighted down, my limbs slow and unresponsive. There was a distant beeping, a rhythmic sound that anchored me, and as I managed to blink my eyes open, the first thing I saw was Logan.

He stood in the corner of the room, arms crossed, expression unreadable, but his presence steady and unwavering. The sterile white walls of the hospital room blurred behind him. I wanted to call his name, but my throat felt thick, and my voice was nonexistent.

Then, something else—warmth. Pressure around my hand. My gaze shifted downward, and there was Noah, his fingers curled around mine, his head bowed as if he'd been waiting forever. My chest tightened, not in pain, but because I heard Noah say something, his voice a low hum against the haze in my head. I blinked again.

I'm alive. I can feel his hand. I need to tell him that.

But the words never formed, my mind slipping away before I could force them out.

I SURFACED AGAIN; MY BODY SLUGGISH BUT LESS HEAVY this time. The world was still hazy, but the light in the room was different—softer, warmer. My throat ached, dry and raw, but I managed to move my lips, whispering the thought that had been locked in my head. "I'm alive."

There was a rustling beside me, and I heard voices. Noah. Logan.

Noah's hand squeezed mine, his voice urgent. "What did he say?"

"I don't know," Logan said, closer now.

I tried again. My lips formed the words, but my voice failed me. My chest felt tight, and exhaustion pulled at me. My frustration flared.

"Why isn't he speaking?" Logan's voice sharpened, the protective older brother in him breaking through.

There was another voice now—calm, professional. The doctor. "It's normal. He's still coming out of anesthesia. His body needs time."

I wanted to tell them I was okay and that I could hear them, but the lure of unconsciousness was too strong. Noah's thumb brushed over my knuckles, and Logan hovered close. I felt safe and grounded. The darkness crept in again, and I let it take me under.

THE NEXT TIME I WOKE, THE WORLD WAS LESS FOGGY, AND I had more awareness. My limbs were still heavy, but I could move them, and when I tried to speak, my voice was there—hoarse, but there.

The doctor stood beside my bed, his gaze assessing as he asked me to follow a light with my eyes, to squeeze his fingers. I managed both, sluggish but responsive. My throat was dry, but I forced out words, faint but clear. "I'm alive."

Noah was there, leaning in, his face coming into focus. "What did you say?"

I tried again. This time, my voice came a little stronger. "Alive."

Noah exhaled a breath of relief as his fingers tightened around mine. Standing beside him, Logan ran a hand down his face before looking at the doctor. "Is he okay?"

The doctor nodded, his expression reassuring. "He's coming around well. No signs of complications. We'll keep monitoring, but this is exactly what we want to see."

I wanted to sit up.

"How about we sit you up?" the doctor asked, his voice even—had I said that out loud? Before I could respond, Noah and Logan were already moving, adjusting the pillows, hands steady as they helped me move.

"It's day two," Noah said as he smoothed the sheet over my legs. His voice was warm. "You're okay, Brody. Everything is okay."

I let out a slow breath, my body exhausted, but my heart steady. Noah's hand was still in mine, solid and sure. I believed him.

. . .

"HAVE YOU TOLD HIM?" LOGAN'S VOICE BROKE THROUGH the quiet hum of the hospital room.

"Not yet," Noah responded, and I wanted to know what they hadn't told me.

"Wha…" I managed.

Noah leaned in. "Hey, you."

"Told. Me. What."

"When you get out of here, we're staying with Logan," Noah clarified, his tone gentle but firm. "Not going back to our place."

I wanted to protest, to say I was fine, but the truth was, I wasn't sure how long I'd even been in the hospital. "How long… here?"

Noah squeezed my hand. "They said another day, maybe two. Just to be sure."

I sighed, nodding. Maybe I wasn't quite ready to argue. Maybe, *just maybe*, letting them take care of me wasn't the worst thing.

"What then?" I asked.

"What?"

"After I can leave Logan's, where will I go?"

"Where will *we* go," Noah corrected. "We'll work it out."

"Together."

"Of course."

We kissed then, and I heard Logan make his excuses until it was only me and Noah in the room. He shifted beside me, his fingers still wrapped around mine. He hesitated, then squeezed my hand. "I've made that decision for us—it's where you'll be safe, and when I return to Harrisburg, you'll have people there with you."

"Not stayin'… Logan… long."

He smiled. "No, not for long."

I concentrated hard. "I want to be with you."

He kissed my nose. "And I want you."

THE DOOR SLAMMED OPEN SO HARD IT RATTLED AGAINST the wall, my grandfather storming in, his face twisted in fury. My security guy gripped his arm, his expression tight, ready to remove him.

"I'm his grandfather!" he barked, his voice echoing in the sterile hospital room.

I barely had the strength to lift my hand, but I managed to nod, a silent command to let him through. Still, I gestured for security to stay close. He might have forced his way in, but I wouldn't be alone. Not completely.

He stopped at the foot of my bed, his gaze raking over me, taking in the hospital gown, the wires, the dullness in my eyes. I could see the moment realization struck, the confirmation he was looking for settling into his rigid posture. "So, it's true," he said, his voice thick with disappointment.

I stared at him, waiting. For what, I wasn't sure. Some words of encouragement? Doubtful. An ounce of concern? Even less likely. But I couldn't force words from my throat, not when my body still felt like it was recovering from being torn apart.

His lip curled, disgust in his expression. "You're broken," he spat. "Worthless to me. Apparently, you're queer? Jesus. A waste of my time."

The words should have hurt. Maybe a few months ago,

they would have. But now, they didn't touch me, sliding off like water. I'd expected nothing more from him. Still, the venom in his voice, the sheer disdain in his eyes, twisted something inside me, a final severing of whatever fragile tie had remained.

Logan's voice was a snarl as he stepped forward, shoving between us, rigid with fury. "You are a hateful, small, pathetic excuse for a man."

Grandfather's eyes flicked to him, looking quite unimpressed. "I don't give a shit what you think. You were never the one I invested in. You were never worth the time."

Logan let out a sharp, bitter laugh. "And look where that got you. You wasted all your time, effort, and manipulation—on what? On someone you could control? Someone you could mold into the second coming of you?"

Grandfather's jaw clenched, his hands curling into fists. "I built this family. I gave him everything when your worthless excuse for a father messed everything up."

"You used him," Logan shot back. "You used all of us. You treat people like tools, like pawns in some game you think you're winning, but guess what? You lost. You lost us all."

The old man's face darkened, and for a second, I thought he might lunge at Logan and spit more venom, but then he turned back to me. His expression was empty of warmth. "Well, you're no use to me now."

He turned on his heel and walked out, his steps sharp, measured, final.

The room was silent except for my ragged breathing.

Logan vibrated with rage; his hands clenched at his sides. The tension was suffocating.

I swallowed and tried to force words past the tightness in my throat. "G-good riddance," I stuttered, my voice hoarse and uneven.

Logan turned to me, his expression relaxing. He exhaled, running a hand down his face before sitting at my bedside. "Yeah," he muttered. "Good fucking riddance."

Noah came in, two coffees—one for him, one for Logan—and a lemon Jell-O Cup for me. My favorite flavor. Who knew I'd have a favorite Jell-O in the hospital?

"What did I miss?" he asked Logan, then stared at me. "Brody?"

"N-nothing 'portant."

"Tell me."

So, Logan told him, and I think he needed my hug as much as I needed his.

THE NEXT DAY, WORDS MADE MORE SENSE IN MY HEAD, and I must've been making sense to others because Noah was smiling a lot and tension had eased in Logan.

Avery had just left, and I was still smiling after she'd sat on my bed and told me a story.

"Do you want kids?" Noah asked when we were alone.

I turned my head to look at him, his expression open, vulnerable. "What do you mean?"

"The future. I mean, I've always had a plan," Noah admitted, his voice steady. "Hockey, kids, family, marriage, a home with my partner." He didn't fumble over his words; he knew what he wanted. Did *I* know what I wanted? "But we've never talked about our forever."

"I never thought I'd have one," I managed to say. I'd grown up with people dying in motorsport. I had the thing in my head. I'd always imagined I'd die young. Noah's eyes brightened with emotion, and I swallowed past the sudden lump in my throat. "Now... I-I have... rest of my life."

"With me," Noah said with a nod.

"Of course." We exchanged smiles. "Kids?" I said.

Noah nodded without hesitation. "My sisters were adopted. I want that too. I want to create my own found family. Maybe surrogacy as well. And dogs. As many dogs as my dad has. I want a house we can fill with everything that matters. I want you."

Emotion thickened his voice, his eyes searching mine, waiting for a response.

I exhaled slowly. I'd never thought about it. I'd never imagined a future beyond racing. It was always about the following season, the next race, the next championship. There was never room for anything else. Noah's grip tightened.

I thought about it. *Really* thought about it. For the first time, I let myself picture a life that wasn't only about speed and trophies. I imagined a house that wasn't a sterile penthouse or a temporary place between races. I imagined a yard filled with dogs; a home filled with laughter. Kids.

I tugged on his hand, motioning for him to sit beside me on the bed. He moved without question, curling into my side, and I wrapped my arm around him, pulling him close. His warmth, his certainty—it settled something in me.

"I want... children," I whispered. "Dogs. Big house... for family. I want you."

Noah pressed his face against my shoulder, his arms winding around me. "Then, that's what we'll have," he murmured. "We'll make it happen. Together."

I kissed the top of his head, inhaling his scent. "We can have that?"

Noah lifted his head to look at me, his expression fierce and unwavering. "Yeah. We can, and I want it with you, Brody. Every single part of it."

I swallowed hard, my chest tight, but in a way that felt full, rather than constricting. "I'm not... running... from e-everything."

He smiled, soft and knowing. "Good. Because I'm not letting you run anymore."

I held him closer, letting his words sink in, allowing the idea of a future to take root in my mind for the first time.

We sat like that for a while holding each other, and neither of us needed to say anything more. We already knew.

THE PRIVATE AMBULANCE RIDE HOME WAS QUIET. THE HUM of the tires on the pavement lulled me into a strange in-between state, where I felt awake, but not fully present. Noah sat beside me, his hand on my knee, steady and grounding. Logan rode up front, making calls and handling things I didn't have the energy to process yet.

Noah only had one more day before returning to Harrisburg for one last practice and a home game against a Washington team.

I sat on the sofa, Avery curled up on my lap, her tiny body warm and heavy against me. She was supposed to be in bed, but I'd used my operation as leverage, claiming I wanted her to stay. Apparently, I could get away with anything for now.

The Washington game played on the TV; the arena alive with energy. Noah stood out even on the small screen, his skating fluid, his focus intense. The cameras lingered on him more than once, the commentators talking about the rookie season, his famous dads, and, of course, his new relationship—his boyfriend, who used to date Jemima Wren. I rolled my eyes at that.

Noah struck in the third period with the Railers up by a single goal—a perfect shot, clean and fast, hitting the net with a satisfying snap. The commentators erupted in excitement.

Four-two, Railers.

I tried to stay calm, but my heart pounded as the seconds ticked. When the final buzzer sounded—a win—I smiled like an idiot.

Later, with Avery finally in bed, my phone buzzed. Noah's face filled the screen, still flushed from the game, his grin wide and breathless.

"I love you! I love you!" he exclaimed, and his teammates cheered in unison, their voices echoing behind him.

"He loves you!" they all chorused, laughing.

Then, a tall, serious-looking guy stepped into the frame. Jack O'Leary, the captain. He gave a firm nod. "Your boy did good, Brody."

"Can you get us a date with Jemima?" someone called.

There was a chorus of groans. "Shut up, Nik!"

The Railers had two more home games—one against a strong Boston team, another against a relentless Carolina squad. The Railers lost to Boston, but took down Carolina, and while Noah didn't score in either, he was everywhere on the ice. He was disrupting plays, controlling the tempo, and playing the kind of game that made the pundits happy. I was so damn proud. I couldn't love him more.

And soon, he would be coming home.

I WAS WAITING IN THE POOL HOUSE, PACING, RESTLESS. Stan and Erik fussed. Logan fussed.

"I'm okay," I said, exasperated. "I can do this on my own. You can all go."

A car pulled up outside. His dads went out to greet him. Logan pulled me in for a tight hug.

"You're gonna be okay," he said.

I smiled. "Of course I will be."

"Love you, little brother," Logan murmured.

"I love you too," I replied. Then, he was gone, and suddenly, I was alone and waiting—waiting too long!

Then, the door opened, and he was there—curls wild, eyes bright, my sexy, incredible man.

We met in the middle, arms locking, bodies pressing together. We hugged and hugged, and when that wasn't enough, we kissed, whispering our hellos, our I-love-yous… our everything.

He was home. And that was all that mattered.

Epilogue

NOAH

One year later

"Where do you keep the paper plates?"

I nudged Margo aside with my hip, and my sister nudged back. Our playful rivalry turned into a hip-checking battle, which she knew I would win, yet the woman refused to back down. From anything. She was strong—case in point, she'd fought for trans rights since her teenage years and never backed down from the bigots who sought to erase her existence. I loved that she was here on vacation, and we fell seamlessly back into our familiar teasing routine in an instant.

I'd missed her since she'd moved to Japan–still healing from her top surgery–to take a job at an anime studio where she'd met Botan. She was now stupidly happy, totally in love, and trying to pull some illegal moves by looping her arm around my neck.

"Two minutes for trying to slap a totally bogus front headlock takedown," I shouted, slipped from her grip, and tossed a rye bun from the tray of bread, meats, and cheeses at her head.

She swatted it aside, laughing maniacally. "You're lucky I'm in such a good mood or else you'd be kissing that new tile you and King Boo just had installed."

King Boo. Only Margo would pin Brody Vance with the name of a character from *Mario Kart.*

"Yeah, yeah, big talk from a cartoonist," I teased. A Hawaiian roll came rocketing at me. I didn't duck in time. Margo hooted at the direct hit between the eyes. At her high-pitched shout, our two beagles, Tracy and Link, started braying in the backyard. We both snorted in amusement. Brody peeked through the kitchen window, his dark eyes bright and clear. The only lingering signs of his fight with the aneurysm and the craniotomy were a bit of blurry vision on occasion and a scar on his scalp where no hair would grow. He grew his hair longer and had it styled to cover the area. "Hey, baby!"

"The show is about to start. Do you two need help carrying out the food, or refereeing the wrestling match?" He smiled through the screen as the dogs ran in circles barking. The rescue twins loved to bark. It was a good thing our new house was situated on some big acreage in a nice neighborhood in Mechanicsburg. We loved our new place. A brand-new Devonshire Artisan house sitting on four acres. Four bedrooms, five baths, and a game room. A pool was slated for installation in two months. We'd miss peak swimming season, as it was already late July, but we'd enjoy the hell out of the in-ground pool next summer.

The dogs adored the grounds, but we had to install an

invisible fence, as beagles, we quickly learned, put their noses to the ground and off they went no matter how loudly you called them back. And someday, our kids will love it. Our house, not the invisible fence. The schools here were good, the neighbors down the road were very accepting of us, and my drive to the rink for games was about ten miles.

"Coming, tell Pops and Dad to chill. Tell Botan to get them some fresh beers from the cooler," Margo told Brody. He nodded, then disappeared.

"You're pretty bossy with my boyfriend," I commented as we pulled dishes of deviled eggs, salads, and a dish of mouthwatering yaki onigiri that Botan had made for his dish to pass. I'd eaten just a few of the fried rice balls because diabetic, but they were to die for.

"Like you haven't been telling Botan what to do for the past two weeks," she countered with a flip of her long, dark hair.

Okay, yeah, that was legit. Botan, Brody, and I had hit it off well, and he'd been helping us with some gardening work. Gardening work meaning playing golf while my sister spent time with our dads. She and my eldest sister didn't get to see them much, so she was spending every moment she could with them before flying back to Japan next week.

"I wish Eva could have made it for the concert," Margo said wistfully as we hoisted platters of food from the counters.

"Yeah, me too, but she's far too pregnant to fly," I replied while heading into the backyard through the screen door in the laundry room. The dogs bounded over, keen noses picking up the aroma of food before we were even out the door properly.

"Pops and Dad are going to be the best grandpas ever. They're driving to Seattle for the birth because of the enormous amount of baby shit they have to deliver," she called over her shoulder.

Yeah, I'd watched the mountain grow over the past nine months. The drive sounded romantic to me. Maybe Brody and I could buy a motorhome and spend my summers off, with the dogs of course, seeing America. I'd much sooner see him behind the wheel of a Winnebago, than that damned Ferrari he sped around Harrisburg in, and the nearby motor speedway in York Haven hitting the track at stupid speeds. Guess we both liked dangerous sports.

"Hey, hey, are we late?" Logan called as he and his little family rushed through the side gate, toting more dishes. "Avery lost her signed Railers cap, so we spent half an hour searching for it. Found it under the fridge."

"I think ghosts put it there," Avery shouted–as she tended to do outside because that was where outdoor voices belonged–while charging to her Uncle Brody for hugs. Which he always gave along with loud smooches that made her giggle.

"If you have ghosts, I know a special way to make them go bye-bye," Pops spoke up from his lawn chair, placed strategically in front of the outdoor projector screen. "What you do is slice potato in half, spit into the air four times–one spit for each direction on compass–and then, you bury potato in garden."

Dad looked at him with skepticism, but said nothing

and, instead, smiled at the man he adored, in that tender way he had.

"My grandfather throws roasted soybeans at the front door while shouting for the demons to be gone, and then, inviting fortune in," Botan added as we took our seats.

"See, is good to use foods for bad spirit leavings no matter what country." Pops nodded. We hurried to get plates heaped, then sat down in a semicircle.

"Oh, it's starting! Oh, my great gods. I love Jemima Wren so much!" Margo fangirled as the worldwide streaming event kicked off. We all knew she loved Jem. It was apparent from the Jem Wren shirt, shorts, socks, sandals, and barrettes she wore.

I wiggled in beside Brody on a swing made for two. He smiled at me, then stole a kiss. I was so happy it almost seemed like a dream. My rookie year had been amazing. We'd made it to the second round of the playoffs, losing to Washington in a seven-game series. My line had been productive both defensively and offensively. The fourth line was often looked down on, but if it could contribute, then the fans and press embraced it. I was training nearly every day, taking care of myself, and working a strict regimen for my diabetes. Life was perfect.

The Railers might make it to the finals next year. We were missing a couple of elements on the top lines, but I was confident that management would do some shopping over the summer to fill those gaps.

"You look so happy," Brody whispered in my ear as he used a finger to push a few curls out of the way.

"I am. I love having our families here."

"Yeah, so do I." He kissed my ear, which made me shiver.

"AHH!! It's Jem and Traci!! Oh, look at them! Are they the most beautiful couple you ever saw?!" Margo was on her feet as Jem and her girlfriend hit the stage with the rest of her band and dancers in Sydney, Australia. Jem and Traci, one of her backup dancers, had announced their relationship about two months ago. The world had gone crazy for about two weeks, stirring up some renewed interest in Brody that faded once the gossip-mongers couldn't get him to sass off about his ex. He was thrilled for Jem. He had a good homelife filled with love, laughter, and family, so why would he badmouth her? Add in lots of speedway-related charity work as well. I refused to think about that damn Ferrari parked in our garage.

I snuggled in close, balancing my plate on my thighs, and let the warm summer day wash over me.

I could think of no better place to be than at Brody's side, living our best lives.

Together.

THE END

What's next in the Railers Legacy series?

Blitz (Railers Legacy 2)

When hockey's hardest hitter meets football's golden boy, sparks fly, and defenses crumble.

Cole "Trick" Harrington III has made a career out of pretending he doesn't care. Not about his past, his name, or the father who built a megachurch empire off judgment and control. Trick torched every bridge back to Atlanta, deliberately wrecked his career, and buried his truth so deep even he started to forget it. Now traded to the Harrisburg Railers, he's skating on thin ice, with a reputation for arrogance and a career teetering on the edge. The last thing he needs is a PR stunt tying him to a squeaky-clean football star, particularly one who is sexy, strong, and always freaking happy. As Trick is forced to confront his growing attraction and deal with the past he's spent years ignoring—including the younger sister he never knew existed—he realizes that the most brutal battles aren't fought on the ice. They're fought in the heart. And this time, he has to stop running.

Tom Fulkowski has led a charmed life. Starting with a typical middle-class childhood in Philly, his skill at catching quarterbacks has propelled him to the heights of pro football. He's got the rings, he's got the cash, and he's got the cars. He's also got a bad back, achy knees, and a yearning to move on. With one final season to play with the Philadelphia Pumas before retirement, Phil looks forward to that next phase of his life. He's just not sure what the next phase is exactly. Then, out of the blue, he meets a wild-eyed hockey player with a chip the size of the Liberty Bell on his shoulder. As he and Cole grow closer, he finds a depth to the younger man that resonates deeply. If only Cole would slow down and let Phil catch up to him, they might win it all.

Blitz is an MM romance featuring a bad-boy hockey player with a past he can't outrun, a football legend on the verge of retirement, a forced PR stunt that might turn into something real, and a game-changing journey to their happy-ever-after.

Hockey Series' from RJ Scott & V.L. Locey

Harrisburg Railers

Owatonna U Hockey

Arizona Raptors

Boston Rebels

LA Storm

Chesterford Coyotes - Young Adult

Railers Legacy

When hockey wunderkind Tennant Rowe meets his new coach, he knows he's in trouble. Jared Madsen is nine years older than Tennant, impossibly attractive, and — worst of all — his brother's off-limits best friend. Is their chemistry worth the risk?

Changing Lines (Railers 1)

Can Tennant show Jared that age is just a number, and that love is all that matters?

The Rowe Brothers are famous hockey hotshots, but as the youngest of the trio, Tennant has always had to play against his brothers' reputations. To get out of their shadows, and against their advice, he accepts a trade to the Harrisburg Railers, where he runs into Jared Madsen. Mads is an old family friend and his brother's one-time teammate. Mads is Tennant's new coach. And Mads is the sexiest thing he's ever laid eyes on.

Jared Madsen's hockey career was cut short by a fault in his heart, but coaching keeps him close to the game. When Ten is traded to the team, his carefully organized world is thrown into chaos. Nine years his junior and his best friend's brother, he knows Ten is strictly off-limits, but as soon as he sees Ten's moves, on and off the ice, he knows that his heart could get him into trouble again.

Harrisburg Railers (Hockey Romance)

1. Changing Lines
2. First Season
3. Deep Edge
4. Poke Check
5. Last Defense
6. Goal Line
7. Neutral Zone
8. Hat Trick
9. Save The Date
10. Baby Makes Three
11. Rivals
12. Perfect Gifts
13. Family First

Railers Volume 1 | Railers Volume 2 | Railers Volume 3 | Railers Volume 4

Meet the men of Owatonna University's hockey team

Ryker (Owatonna U, 1)

Ryker is hockey royalty, Jacob is a poor country boy. Can two vastly different people find common ground and become the men they want to be?

Ryker comes from a long line of championship-winning hockey players. Playing college hockey to develop his game is his only focus, and nothing will stand in the way of him working to become the best player. He has no room for relationships, people who point out his flaws, or anyone who calls him on his dreams. He certainly has no place for love, and meeting Jacob is nothing but a useful distraction on the side. After all trying to get his Owatonna Eagles teammate into bed is less work and more play. When tragedy rocks his family, his charmed life crumbles, and the only person he can turn to is the same one who claims to hate him.

Jacob Benson has only known hard work and stifling conservative values his whole life. Born and raised in the small rural community of Eden Crossing, Minnesota, he's the only son of a hard-working but struggling dairy farming family. Jacob is using his skills in hockey to finance his way to an agricultural science degree. These four years at Owatonna U. will probably be the only time he has to enjoy life, gain acceptance about his sexuality, and live openly before his inevitable return to the farm. Running into a pretty rich boy like Ryker Madsen is putting a damper on his enjoyment of life away from home. Ryker's flip, conceited, carefree attitude grates on Jacob's every nerve. So why, if Ryker is everything he dislikes, does he want nothing more than to explore the sinful dreams that his annoying teammate stars in every night?

Ryker

Owatonna U Hockey (Hockey Romance)

1. Ryker
2. Scott
3. Benoit
4. Christmas Lights
5. Valentine's Hearts
6. Desert Dreams

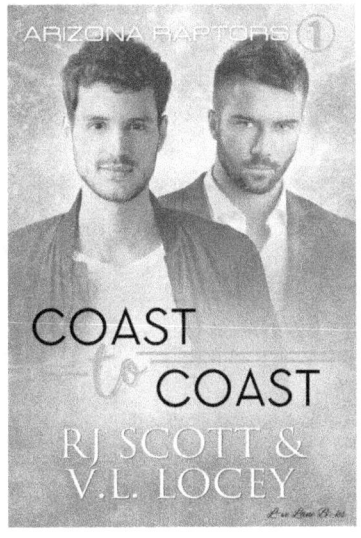

Coast to Coast (Arizona Raptors 1)

Coast To Coast

**When opposites attract, this bottom-of-the-league team will
never be the same again.**

A stipulation in his father's will forces Mark back into the arms of
a family that disowned him and leaves him one-third owner of a
hockey team facing financial ruin. He doesn't even watch hockey,
let alone like it, and wants nothing more than to head back to
New York. Then there's the new coach, a stubborn, opinionated,
irritating man with superiority issues and questionable music

taste. Butting heads with Rowen becomes the new normal, but it comes with passionate debate and an all-consuming lust.

Challenged to rebuild one of the worst teams in the league into a future cup contender, Rowen can't pass up the opportunity. Never in his twenty years of hockey has he ever seen a team managed so badly or coached players overflowing with resentment and bigotry. Yet there's something about this team and this city that compels him to roll up his sleeves and start dismantling. If only Mark, one of three siblings who now own the Raptors, wasn't so damned rock-headed yet so damned appealing his job might be easier. It doesn't look like either is willing to give in, but one night in a dark, desert hotel changes everything.

Coast To Coast

Arizona Raptors (Hockey Romance)

1. Coast To Coast
2. Across the Pond
3. Shadow and Light
4. Sugar and Ice
5. School and Rock

Boston Rebels

Top Shelf (Boston Rebels 1)

Acting on the attraction to his best friend's brother has always been off the table for Xander until a passionate hookup with Mason at a beach resort begins a love affair that burns long after summer ends.

Mason specializes in assisting same-sex couples on their journey to becoming parents and fighting every rule that blocks his way in the stuck-in-the-past agency that hired him. Living in his brother's pool house is rent-free, and every cent he earns he saves for his dream—that one day he'd have his own company helping others. The downside is that he has to see his annoying brother every day, the upside is that his brother's teammates from the

Boston Rebels make regular visits. The eye candy that passes Mason's window is almost enough to make him consider dating a hockey player, but not just any player though. Ever since Xander —his brother's childhood friend—came out as gay at a press conference, Mason's puppy love has turned into a burning attraction he can no longer ignore.

Hockey has been one of Xander's main focuses since he was old enough to balance on skates. Well, hockey and Mason Kingsley, but Mason was always unattainable. Now that he's about to see thirty candles on his birthday cake and is no longer hiding the fact he's gay, he's ready to find a soul mate to make his life complete. A summer vacation is just what he needs to have time to think, but when the Boston Rebels arriving in paradise with Mason in tow, thinking is the last thing he needs. One torrid night under a balmy moon and rules about not messing with his best friend's brother vanish on a warm, tropical breeze.

Summer romances don't generally last past Labor Day, but with the new season about to begin Xander and Mason are going to have to face the world and decide if their love is real enough to withstand everything.

———

Boston Rebels

Lost In Boston (Free Prequel Novella)

1. Top Shelf
2. Back Check
3. Snowed
4. Royal Lines
5. Blade
6. Rental

LA Storm

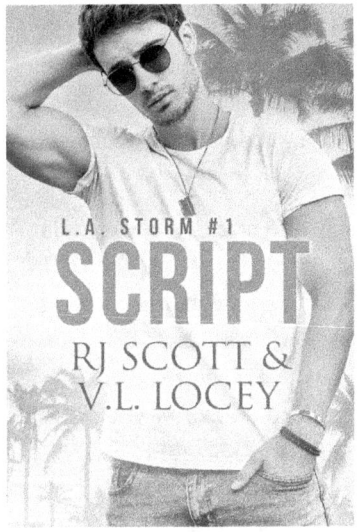

Script (LA Storm, 1)

Script

Hollywood A-lister Finn might be Canadian, but he needs Cameron to show him how to hockey.

Actor Finn Kerrigan is at a crossroads. After growing up a soap star, then starring in a hugely successful trilogy of action movies, he's finally given the chance to read a heartfelt and passionate script that could change his life forever. The role would be enough for people to see him as a serious actor, and maybe even win him an award or two (and no, a golden raspberry award for his action movies doesn't count). Once established as a serious actor he's sure he can come out of the closet and finally live his truth. When he lies to get the part of a hockey player on a struggling team, he suddenly has nowhere to hide. He might be Canadian, but the last time he skated he was ten, and no, he doesn't have hockey in his blood. With only a month until filming starts, he about to be exposed, but partnered with a player who's supposed to be giving him tips, he doesn't realize how many of his secrets will come to light. Falling in lust, one heated kiss at a time, is inevitable, but giving Cameron up at the end of the shoot could break his heart.

Cameron Chavkin is the face of the LA Storm. And the body, and the hair, and the smile. He's at the prime of his career, men and women want to be with him, and he's skating better than he ever has before. His house sits next to a famous rock star's mansion, his garage is filled with expensive cars, and he's even been asked to mentor a once-famous actor in a new hockey movie. Life is pretty sweet. Until the bad boy of hockey meets Finn, a man on the edge with more secrets than Cameron has endorsements.

Knowing better than to get involved, Cameron is swept up despite himself, and when it's time to say goodbye to the Storm's most eligible bachelor is finding it hard to follow the script.

Script

LA Storm

1. Script
2. Second
3. Shield
4. Spiral

Speed (Railers Legacy 1)

Hard ice. Fast cars. Fierce love.

And a race against fate.

Hockey is as natural as breathing for Noah. Growing up with two famous hockey stars as his dads, Noah has always aspired to join the Railers to continue the Lyamin-Gunnarsson legacy. With his degree done, it's time to live that dream, and the first step is being drafted by the team his hall-of-fame dad played for. The second step is to pull on that dusky blue-gray sweater and make his fathers proud. His rookie year is bound to be a season of incredible highs and lows, but one of the biggest highlights is meeting Brody Vance at a fundraiser. Brody is the living epitome of a bad boy hiding his pain behind a devil-may-care attitude. As Noah struggles to keep one eye on the puck and not on Brody, it's only a matter of time before both loves collide in a chaotic splash of media attention.

Bad boy racing driver Brody has spent his life chasing speed and glory and is only points away from his first world championship when a devastating crash ends his season. Determined to make a triumphant comeback, Brody is blindsided by a diagnosis that forces him off the track for good. With his world flipped upside down and family and fans questioning why he left, Brody hides his pain by pushing the limits and refusing to let anyone see the cracks. But after a chance meeting with a sweet, sexy hockey player turns into an unforgettable one-night stand, fate keeps putting Noah in his path. With his heart on the line and his body racing against time, Brody must decide if he's willing to risk it all for love—or if he'll let fear and pride leave him in the dust.

Speed is a steamy M/M romance with a hockey rookie living his family legacy, a bad-boy racing driver with secrets, media attention that would break even the strongest of men, an unforgettable one-night stand, a love that means risking it all, and a hard-won happily ever after.

Railers Legacy

1. *Speed*
2. *Blitz*
3. *Powder*
4. *Fly*

Chesterford Coyotes, Young Adult
Romance

Off The Ice (Chesterford Coyotes, 1)

Off The Ice

A coming-of-age love story with high school, hockey rivalry, friendship, family, and coming out.

Soren's life changes in an instant when he and his younger brother are adopted by hockey royalty. Making sense of his new life is hard enough, but when he's enrolled in a private school it means facing a whole new set of problems. Navigating friendship, family, and hockey is one thing, but being attracted to the boy who vexes him is a whole new thing.

Felix has a reputation to protect. He's the kid who seems to have everything but looks can be deceiving. Spinning lies about his perfect life, he's created a fantasy world that even he has started to believe. Only, it's not long before everything crumbles, all of his pretty lies are revealed, and only his closest rival sees through his pain and stands by him.

Fighting is easy, friendship is hard, but love is everything.

Off The Ice

Chesterford Coyotes

1. Off The Ice
2. On Thin Ice
3. *Dance on Ice*

Free Reads

Please note - in all of these free stories, there will be some spoilers for the main series books.

Railers Short Stories

Volume 1 | Volume 2

LA Storm

Sparkle

The Colts - AHL Short Stories

Pucks & Percentages

Breakaway

Making the Save

Standalone

Waiting for Christmas

Also By RJ Scott

For a full list of ebooks and links please scan the code above or visit rjscott.co.uk/rjbooks

Meet RJ Scott

RJ discovered romance in books at a very young age and realized that if there wasn't romance on the page, she could create it in her head. With over one hundred and fifty books published, she is a full time author of gay romance.

She lives and works out of her home in the beautiful English countryside, spends her spare time reading, watching films, and enjoying time with her family.

The last time she had a week's break from writing she didn't like it one little bit and has yet to meet a box of chocolates she couldn't defeat.

www.rjscott.co.uk | rj@rjscott.co.uk

Newsletter - gayromance.co.uk/mailing-list

instagram.com/rjscott_author

amazon.com/author/rj-scott

bookbub.com/authors/rj-scott

Also By VL Locey

For a full list of ebooks and links please scan the code above or visit vllocey.com/stories-from-vl-locey

Meet V.L. Locey

V.L. Locey loves worn jeans, yoga, belly laughs, walking, reading and writing lusty tales, Greek mythology, the New York Rangers, comic books, and coffee.

(Not necessarily in that order.)

She shares her life with her husband, her daughter, one dog, two cats, a flock of assorted domestic fowl, and two Jersey steers.

When not writing spicy romances, she enjoys spending her day with her menagerie in the rolling hills of Pennsylvania with a cup of fresh java in hand.

vllocey.com
vicki@vllocey.com

Newsletter - vllocey.com/newsletter

facebook.com/V.L.Locey
x.com/vllocey
instagram.com/vl_locey
bookbub.com/authors/v-l-locey
goodreads.com/vllocey
pinterest.com/vllocey